The man got to her on every level. It just figured she'd been thinking about him all day and her traitor of a best friend had let him into her house.

"Right. There's me." Maggie cleared her throat and tried to move away, but he wouldn't let her. "Um, Mac? Let me go."

"Since you said my name, okay." He released her and stepped back, looking smug.

This Mac Jameson she knew too well. "I say your name all the time."

"When you're not calling me a jerk, a dictator, or an asshole, you usually call me Jameson." He crossed those incredible arms over his massive chest.

She refrained from fanning herself and planted her hands on her hips, wanting to appear strong, not swoony from the sight of his incredible body.

WORKING OUT

BY MARIE HARTE

A No Box Books Publication

ISBN-13: 978-1539150855
Working Out
Copyright © 2016, 2012 by Marie Harte
Cover by Tibbs Design, No Box Books Design
Edited by TINB Inc.

No Box Books

http://marieharte.com

CHAPTER ONE

December in Seattle

HE'D KNOWN IT WAS COMING TO THIS. FOR FOUR LONG-ass months, he'd been doing his best to handle the situation, and for four months he'd been fooling himself.

Mac Jameson gripped the neck of his beer bottle and glared across the bar at the bane of his existence. He could no longer ignore those big blue eyes, that killer rack, or the platinum blond hair that framed a face that haunted his dreams. She worked for him, but it didn't stop her from sniping, scowling, or blatantly ignoring him when she didn't like what he had to say. A smarter man would have taken her signals as uninterested and run the other way.

But not Mac. He thrived on challenge, and Maggie Doran had *dare* written all over her. Aside from her smart mouth and incredible looks, she had a work ethic he truly respected. To make matters worse, she was far from perfect, which he would have found boring. No woman could look like she did without carrying some massive baggage.

He hadn't yet figured out how to unload her issues long enough to sleep with her and put himself out of his misery.

A solid clap to his back reminded him he wasn't drinking alone.

"So what's your excuse this time?" his best friend asked as he joined Mac at the bar. "The redhead not hot enough? The brunette who wanted your number too clingy?"

Mac refused to pay attention to the end of the bar where two sexy women continued to glance at him in between high-pitched laughter and cocktails. "I don't date women who giggle. Christ, I'm thirty-six, too old for games."

"Since when?" Shane, as usual, ignored the scowl Mac shot him and continued to talk. "The Mac I know has no problem serial dating. What was it you said to me not so long ago? To indulge in the holy trinity and forget my problems? Tits, ass and an orgasm. There you go, buddy. You have two more-than-willing candidates still making eyes at you." Shane discreetly nodded toward Mac's new groupies.

"No fault with the trinity. You have me there." Mac had to smile. His grin faded when he noticed his recent obsession now sandwiched between two guys pointing fingers at each other.

Shane followed Mac's attention and sighed. "Figures. That woman is trouble." And Shane would know. Now dating Shelby, Maggie's best friend, Shane spent more time with Maggie than Mac did—a fact that annoyed the crap out of him, not that he'd ever admit it out loud.

"Don't get me wrong. I like her a lot," Shane continued, "but that stupid vow of celibacy is like a neon sign on her forehead. It's like Maggie's secretly calling out to anyone with a dick to help end her plight."

Mac blinked. "What did you say?"

"Oh, sorry. *Plight* means problem. As in, she has

something troubling her."

"Dickhead. No, what you said about her vow of celibacy."

"Oh that. Maggie is off men, or so Shelby told me. I'm sworn to secrecy, so don't say anything." Shane shrugged and drank from his beer. "Oh hell. Looks like I'm going to have to help her out. Those guys don't look like they're playing."

Mac wanted to get back to Maggie's issue about not having sex, but Shane was right. "You stay here in case I need someone to bail me out of jail. I'll handle those guys."

Shane stared at him a moment, then nodded. "Yeah. Just flex a few times and they'll scatter like mice."

Mac shot him a not-so-nice grin.

"And do that. The smile that's more a grimace. Great intimidation factor, there."

In a mood to crack some skulls together, Mac muscled through the crowded bar and reached Maggie in time to hear her telling both guys off.

"… if you'd even bothered to ask, you'd know I never drink tequila. And I don't like grabby men. Period."

When Maggie grew angry, her voice turned huskier, sexier. It put Mac in mind of satin sheets and naked limbs entangled with his. Unfortunately, her voice seemed to have the same effect on the morons fighting over her. Morons that looked somehow familiar.

The redhead poked the dark-haired guy in the belly. Both appeared of equal weight and height, yet neither had the same musculature as Mac. Of the two, the dark-haired man looked meaner, so Mac kept an eye on him.

Maggie turned to the redhead. "Brent, it's okay—"

Brent cut her off. "She's with me, Wilson."

"Yeah, right." Wilson made a face. "Why would she want you when she could have me? I can buy and sell you twice over, and you...what? You own a nice little home in Green Lake and bench press twenty more pounds in the gym? Please."

Brent had patience, because he took a deep breath and let it out without slugging the guy. "Wilson, don't be such a dick. Maggie and I were talking before you interrupted."

"Talking? Brent, she was backing away and trying to be polite about it." Wilson huffed. "Poor thing just doesn't know how to reject you without hurting your feelings."

Mac suddenly realized where he'd seen the men before. They were members of Jameson's Gym—his uncle's pride and joy, and his current employer. It should have made him reconsider his need to pound both of them into tomorrow. Brent had been a member for a few months and wasn't a bad guy, but Wilson was new. He also appeared to be a conceited jerk.

Maggie opened her mouth, no doubt to say something snarky. She might be little, but she didn't tolerate fools well at all. Then she spotted Mac and snapped her mouth closed. The fire in her blue eyes went straight to his gut. Damn, she was pretty, especially when riled.

"Maggie." He smiled through his teeth.

"Oh hell." She groaned.

"I'm hanging with Shane." He nodded back to the bar. "He sent me down here to get you. Said he wants to talk to you." A good enough excuse to pry her away without stirring too much trouble. Mac might be in the mood for a fight, but he didn't relish his uncle riding his ass for screwing with paying customers.

Wilson frowned at him, showing no recognition. "Hey, asshole. I'm busy with the lady. Why don't you go shoot up some more steroids while me and my friend handle this?"

Mac wanted to be a better man and not react to the insult,

but the Marine within, even two years retired, refused to back away from a fight. Especially since numbnuts didn't know better than to insult Mac.

"Hell." Brent sighed. "Hey, Mac. Maggie, it was nice talking to you. I'll catch you later." He turned and walked away.

Which left Wilson sneering. "He might be scared of you, but I'm not."

"Clearly." Mac glanced at Maggie. "You okay? I mean, I wouldn't want to come between you and your newest conquest." As soon as he said it, he wanted to smack himself. For some reason, around this particular woman, he couldn't hold his tongue. The charm he'd been famous for, that had gotten him laid like nobody's business, vanished when in her presence.

"You're as big a jerk as he is." Maggie thumbed her displeasure at Wilson.

"Excuse me?" Wilson turned to her and put a hand on her shoulder. "I know you didn't just call me a jerk—"

Mac didn't think. The minute the bastard put his hand on Maggie, Mac reacted. He took hold of the offending hand on Maggie's shoulder and put Wilson into a wristlock in seconds, forcing the man to his knees.

While Wilson howled in pain and the crowd standing around them suddenly drew back, Mac wondered how far to punish him.

"Jameson, it's okay." Maggie put a hand on his arm. As usual, the contact seared him. "He wasn't bothering me. Well, he was, but it's fine now. I'm sure Wilson just wants to put tonight behind him."

"You got that right, bitch," Wilson muttered.

"Who you calling a bitch, fuckhead?" Mac let his wrist go and grabbed him by the throat. "Apologize to the lady before I crush you."

Wilson choked. A few people nearby who'd heard the insult cheered Mac's efforts, while the chatter around them grew more excited.

Maggie tugged at Mac's arm. "Cut it out. The bouncers are coming over. You'll get in trouble."

She sounded like she cared. He hated that his heart raced because she might.

"Sure thing, sweetcakes." He smiled at her sudden glare. "I'll let him go just as soon as dickhead here apologizes."

"Then maybe you should give him air so he can breathe." She took her hand from him and crossed her arms over her full breasts, clearly outlined in a pretty blue sweater that clung to her curves.

Man, he wanted to see if her sweater was as soft as it looked, and more, if those breasts were a true handful. Mac had big hands, and Maggie had a build that promised to fulfill all his dreams.

Her eyes narrowed when she saw the direction of his gaze.

"Uh, Mac, you need to let him go," Shane said from just behind him. "He's turning purple."

Mac loosened his grip. "Everyone's a critic. Well, Wilson? We're waiting."

Wilson drew in huge breaths of air and stuttered a half-assed apology.

"Great. He's sorry. Now let him go," Maggie ordered.

Mac released Wilson and stepped back, putting himself between the guy and Maggie. "Time to go, friend."

The bouncers arrived. The bigger of the two, who might have proven a true threat if it came down to a fight, grinned at Mac. "Surprise, surprise. You causing problems again, Jameson?"

Mac smiled back at Jonas, a fellow weight-lifter he occasionally worked out with from the gym. "Nah. Dickhead here must have had too much to drink. He was getting a little grabby with Maggie, but I think he decided he's done for the night."

Wilson rubbed his throat and nodded. He glared up at Mac but didn't say a word.

"Good to know." Jonas latched onto Wilson's arm. "Let me help you out. Bill, let's escort Mr. Dickhead to the door." Bill and Jonas walked Wilson out.

Pleased to have dealt with the guy without knocking out all his teeth, Mac turned to Maggie, prepared to receive her gratitude.

Instead, she knocked him in the chest. "What are you *doing?*"

Even in the dim light of the bar, he saw her flush. Man, he hated that she looked even better when embarrassed. As usual, his imagination prodded him to wonder if she looked that pink all over when she blushed.

Shane's chuckle turned to a cough when Maggie included him in her scowl.

"Oh, I'm sorry," Mac replied, overly polite. "Was I supposed to let him feel you up, then drag you back to his place for some fun? You looking to get bent over for a good hard fu—"

She clapped a hand over his mouth. "Don't you *dare* finish that sentence."

"I'm telling Shelby about this later." Shane sounded way too amused.

Maggie threatened, "You do and I'm telling her you were flirting with those girls at the bar. Yeah, I saw you."

"I was not." Shane didn't sound so pleased now.

7

Mac licked the fingers over his mouth, wanting to lick a helluva lot more than that. Man, he loved it when she turned mean.

Maggie whipped her hand away, looking so appealing he had half a mind to throw her over his shoulder and take her somewhere private for the rest of the night. Hell, make that, the rest of the month.

"You are such a Neanderthal."

"Flatterer." Mac winked.

She sighed. "I didn't need your help. I was talking to Brent when that jerk Wilson showed up. I recognized them from the gym, so I didn't think anything about it. They would have walked away if you hadn't—"

"Bent his hand back like a pretzel?" he offered. "Showed him how to behave around women?"

"Stuck your big fat head where it didn't belong." She seethed. Her blond hair fluttered like a halo around her face when she shook her head. "I know you thought you were helping, but I had it all under control."

"Yeah? How? By playing the part of a bone between two hungry dogs? Brent's not so bad, but Wilson is definitely an asshole."

She blew out a breath. "Well, yeah. But you didn't have to be so—"

"Forceful? Manly? Impressive?"

"Intrusive. Domineering. Aggressive," she countered.

"Don't forget obnoxious and brutal," Shane had to add.

Mac flipped him the finger, which only made his best friend laugh.

Maggie groaned. "Is it too much to ask that I have a relaxing night away from Jameson's Gym? Just one."

She had been putting a lot of hours in at work, but only

because so many patrons wanted to take her class. Ever since Maggie had started working for him four months ago, she'd steadily grown her aerobics following from one class once a week to two classes five days a week. And people wanted more.

"Sorry, baby. Want me to rub your shoulders to relax you?" Before she could protest, he put his hands on her, the way he'd been wanting to since he'd seen her appear in the bar. He kept his touch firm but not punishing, and her moan turned him instantly hard.

"Get off me, and don't call me *baby*." Yet she made no move to leave his touch.

"Why not see Shelby for a massage? You look tense," Shane noted.

Mac could vouch for Shane's girlfriend. Shelby continued to work on his knee, and her deep tissue work had actually improved his flexibility. "Yeah, Shelby would help if you asked."

"I'm fine. I know Shelby would help if I asked. I'm her best friend, remember?" Maggie tugged her shoulders away, and Mac grudgingly let her go.

I really need to get laid. Any more time near Maggie Doran and I might explode. He shoved his hands in his pockets and tried to concentrate on willing away his erection. "Hey, if this is because I'm working you too hard, I can always cut back on your hours." He liked her around, but he didn't want to work her to death.

"No. Actually, I need the workouts, and the extra money helps." She rolled her shoulders. "But that wasn't bad, Jameson."

She never called him Mac, and that distance bothered him. "No problem, *Doran*."

"You're good. You should think about going into massage

therapy. Especially given your wonderful way with people."

Shane snorted. "Yeah, like he could really give Shelby a run for her money."

"Ha ha." Mac sneered at Shane before turning his attention back to Maggie. "Don't worry, sweetcakes. I'm not giving up my day job."

"About that," Shane said. "So is your uncle really quitting the gym and leaving it all you or what? He's been saying that for two years."

"Who the hell knows? Ian Jameson is as big a pain in my ass as you are."

"I strive to please."

Maggie snickered and said to Shane, "You are a pain, but a cute one. I've never seen Shelby happier than she's been with you."

Shelby—Maggie's best friend. Yet another reason Mac should end his fascination with the woman. Bad enough Maggie worked for him. She was also best friends with Shane's girlfriend. Too many close ties would turn their relationship to shit when a fling between them ended.

No fling. No relationship. No sex. The woman is trouble. How sad he had to remind himself of that fact daily.

Mac tuned back in to the conversation and heard something about a Christmas party. Feeling less than celebratory after realizing he'd spend another lonely night without female companionship, he got up to order another beer.

The women at the end of the bar waved at him. He nodded back but made no move to engage. Since the day he'd first laid eyes on her, Mac's desire burned for one woman and one woman only.

Freakin' Maggie Doran.

He was doomed.

CHAPTER TWO

MAGGIE SPENT THE NEXT WEEK DOING HER BEST TO avoid Mac. For the past four and a half months, she'd been on a no-man diet. Though celibacy wasn't fun, it also wasn't as annoying as the many losers she seemed to attract. Except her boss had been keeping her awake at night. Fantasies about the man tempted her to cave in to her desires and try him on for size. Talk about a colossal mistake.

In an effort to stop thinking about him and return to her fun-loving self, she'd arranged a date with her best friend. Tonight, she finally had Shelby to herself again. Though Maggie loved that her friend was finally dating a decent guy, she missed their Friday night movies.

She smiled at Shelby over Shelby's kitchen counter, bemused to see her friend so carefree and happy. "Shane is good for you."

Shelby's brown eyes glowed with humor. "I thought we were doing a girls' night. No boys or boy-talk allowed."

"Right."

"Yet you bring up he-who-must-not-be-named." Shelby's

grin turned sly. "Oh wait, that's not Shane. That's studly Mac Jameson, your secret crush."

Maggie made a face.

"Oh yeah. I've seen the way you look at him. The same way he looks at you. You *like* him."

"Girls' night. Quit breaking the rules." Maggie reached for her margarita and took a sip. "Oh man, I needed that."

"You need more than a drink, I'm thinking. You poor, born-again virgin. Go out and get laid, isn't that what you told me before? You know, when I was all pathetic and sad?"

"Don't pity me. We had a deal to be cat ladies *together*. The pain of your betrayal wounds. Truly."

Shelby laughed. "Dream on. Before Shane, I was going to be happily alone forever. No cats, dogs, kids, men, nothing but my mother and Ron to nag me into an early grave."

"At least you would have had Mimi and Ron. I just have Trevor, and I can't keep track of him." Maggie's brother spent as much time abroad as he did stateside. Like she really believed his bull about working for a shipping company when the government signed his paychecks.

"And speaking of Trevor, is he coming home for Christmas? Because I thought you were spending the day with us." *Us* meant Shelby, Shane, Shelby's mother and Ron. Shelby's mother put the E in eccentricity, but she had a heart made of gold. Mimi and Shelby's surrogate father, Ron, made an unstoppable team. The odd pair had pseudo-adopted Maggie years ago, for which she'd always be grateful.

Maggie sighed. "The last time I spoke to big brother, he planned to come home by mid-March. Nope. You're stuck with me for Christmas." Maggie glanced past her and gaped in horror at the calendar on the wall. "Hell. That's in just three more weeks."

Marie Harte

"Yeah. Better get moving, slacker." Shelby smirked. "I've already done *my* shopping."

"That's because you're anal retentive. And your boyfriend is as big a planner as you are. You two are so annoying together, it's sickening."

Shelby sighed. "It is, isn't it?"

Maggie guzzled her margarita. "We need little umbrellas to be more festive. And we're done talking about men."

"Fine by me. Oh, here are the mozzarella sticks." Shelby turned off the oven and took the tray out. She stared from them to Maggie and frowned. "I'll have to run an extra mile or two this weekend because of tonight. Sometimes I hate that you're blond, gorgeous, and eat like a horse. You should be as big as a house but look like a perpetual size two."

"I work out or I would be a house." Maggie popped a nearby chip and sighed with pleasure. "These are so bad for me." She turned to grab a mozzarella stick and bobbled the hot treat onto her plate.

"Chips and deep fried cheese. That rung on the food pyramid no one wants to talk about. Between this crap and the sugar content in our margaritas, we're batting a thousand." Shelby groaned. "But it all tastes so good. Now let's go watch *Avatar.*"

"For the sixth time," Maggie complained under her breath.

"I heard that. And it's the fifth time."

"I thought we were back on horror movies."

"Nope. Sci-Fi. So shut up, sit back, and be enthralled by blue people with tails."

Maggie tried, but halfway through the film she found her thoughts continually straying to Mac and staying there. She'd been so turned on when he'd mauled Wilson last week. He'd been so forceful and sexy while protecting *her*. Of course she'd

14

gotten a rush seeing him in action. Any woman would, and Maggie happened to like muscles on a man.

Her practical side reared its head, insisting that she courted stupidity to work for a man like Mac when she didn't actually need to. She had her fulltime job at the gallery. On top of that, her old gym missed her and continually asked when she might return. They had better hours and were closer to home. So why didn't she stop working her *temporary* job for Mac and focus more on her real career? How had she gotten in so deep with the aggravating man she wanted to punch as much as she wanted to kiss?

She glanced at Shelby—the real reason for her current dilemma.

Four months ago, she'd tried to help her idiotic best friend. Out to protect Shelby from making another mistake when it came to men, Maggie had taken a job at Mac's gym. While trying to spy on Shane, she'd ended up conspiring with Mac to get Shelby and Shane together.

Over the course of Maggie's time spent plotting, she'd started to actually like the man that put the word *testosterone* to shame. Mac stood a few inches over six feet, making him a giant next to her. He swore like the Marine he'd once been, yet he also charmed the ugly out of the nastiest woman at the gym with little effort. He had his share of fan-girls in leotards and short shorts. Big-breasted, slutty Megan thought Mac could do no wrong. And according to gossip, Mac definitely knew what to do between the sheets.

Apparently he couldn't hold down a relationship though, much to the chagrin of several gym-goers who liked to stare at Mac and speculate. As much as she wanted to, Maggie couldn't blame their interest. Mac fit every one of her ideal physical traits in a male. Tall, broad shouldered and thickly muscled, he had looks and charm—when he chose to use it. His square jaw framed an even grin that made her heart race whenever he flashed it. Bright blue eyes against tan skin contrasted with his thick black hair. He kept it short but a little long in the front, and she had a constant urge to brush his bangs off his forehead, to touch him and see if—

"I love this part." Shelby knocked her in the arm, and Maggie watched as the end fight broke out in earnest.

Oh, hell. I have to stop mooning over Mac Jameson. She got up to pour herself another drink as the credits rolled. Shelby joined her, and they argued the finer points of science fiction versus horror movies.

Before she knew it, she and Shelby had finished off the pitcher of margaritas and started talking about men. Again.

"And when I wanted to do something different, he met me halfway." Shelby nodded happily and under her shirt, muscled out of her bra. "Sorry. But it's been a long day, and I've earned it. I'm free-boobing."

A good idea. Maggie wanted to take hers off as well, except Shane would at some point return. Despite her supposed appeal to the opposite sex, Maggie had a hard time bearing her assets to the world.

Shelby tossed her bra and sighed. "Much better. Oh Maggie, I am so gone for him. I have to remind myself to play hard to get, because I don't want him to get bored. Sometimes I have a hard time believing I'm in a real relationship. We're actually dating. I mean, I love him. Isn't that weird?"

Maggie snorted. "And we're back to talking about Shane. Wait a minute. You said you have to remind yourself to play hard to get? You? The man smiles at you and you drop your pants like Pavlov's dog."

"Huh? Dogs wear pants?"

"I meant…never mind." She wasn't exactly sure what she meant. The margaritas were finally kicking in. "So what do you think about Mac?"

"Ha! I knew you were still thinking about him." Shelby sounded a bit too rational, and Maggie realized she'd imbibed much more than her friend.

Time for Shelby to catch up.

She retrieved a half full bottle of wine from the refrigerator and poured two cups, then rejoined Shelby in the living room and handed her one. "Drink up, schoolgirl."

Shelby accepted the glass. "Mac's in major lust with you."

Which made it so difficult to keep her distance. Maggie called him Jameson. She frowned and glared, keeping a tight watch on his many ex-girlfriends to remind herself she didn't want to join their ranks.

"And *you* want *him*, bad." Shelby refused to shut up. "But that might be because you're so asexual now."

Maggie groaned and drank. She had been doing her best not to talk about her lack of a sex life, but the booze and need to share broke her restraint. "I know. At first it was hard, but now it's getting easier to not want sex." *At least, when I'm not around Mac. And that scares me.* "I'm almost thirty. What's going to happen when I'm in my forties and fifties? All my good years will be gone, and I'll go through the change and never want sex again. I'll be a dried up has-been."

"Not to hear my mother tell it."

"I love Mimi."

"Yeah, well, she talks too much." Shelby winced. "Trust me. She way over-shares. But here's a good thing. She told me that since I've found a man she finally approves of, she's decided to work on *your* sorry love life. She and Ron are going to find you the perfect man."

A vision of Mac wearing a white towel and not much else danced across Maggie's vision. "Great. I suppose this is payback for me helping you find your true love."

"Yep."

"You don't have to look so gleeful about it." Maggie frowned. "I mean, you got Shane out of the deal. You owe me."

Shelby smirked. "Oh, I intend to pay you back. In spades."

"Hell."

Shelby chuckled. "I've been feeling up your obsession for weeks now."

Maggie huffed. "He's not my obsession. And might I remind you that you're a professional. I thought legitimate massage therapists were more clinical about their patients."

"Well, I'm not giving him happy endings. Those I save for my man."

Maggie snorted with laughter. "You need help."

"And I get it regularly." Shelby wiggled her eyebrows. "Did I tell you about Shane *helping* me out at work? God, that man is sexy."

Maggie stared, wide-eyed. "By helping out, you mean…"

"He had me naked and splayed out on a table. My own personal massage."

"You, Miss Professional, had sex in your clinic? Oh man, I am so jealous. Tell me."

As Shelby shared a few naughty details, like the good best friend she was, Maggie felt both stunned and envious of her friend. Shane had certainly brought out the adventurous girl in Shelby, and it was about time. Shelby had been so hurt by her ex that it had soured Maggie on relationships as well. Shelby's pleasure showed Maggie that not all men were scum-sucking jerks.

Maggie longed to have someone to trust, to fill her emotional and physical needs and validate her sense as a woman. For so long she'd tried dating men who turned out to be all wrong, and those mistakes triggered a fear that she'd never find someone special. She had looks but no great wealth, and someday her looks would fade. Most men didn't take her seriously because of her blond hair and dream to be an artist. Even in this day and age, stereotypes remained. For all that men complimented her face and form, she had yet to find a significant other.

"...so then he flipped me over, and I'm all out of breath, and he—"

The front door opened, cutting Shelby off mid-sentence. Shane walked in and stopped short at seeing them both lolling on the floor with a bottle of wine between them. He stared hard at Shelby, who wore a pair of tights and a tank without her bra. Then he blinked at Maggie, who wore her favorite ripped jeans and a soft, holey tee-shirt.

"Please tell me I didn't miss any girl-on-girl action."

Shelby laughed so hard she knocked the empty bottle over.

Maggie got to her feet with the grace of a three-legged goat. She nearly tripped before Shane steadied her. "And this is why I kept my bra on."

He stared, open-mouthed, but said nothing. The looks he kept giving Shelby spoke for him, however.

"Okay, you two." Maggie sighed. "I don't think I can drive home. So I'll be in the guest room. Please, no loud noises while you're getting it on. Have pity on me." So saying, she teetered her way to the bathroom, took care of business, and then found the bed in the guest room.

After three tries, she shimmied out of her bra and jeans but kept her shirt on for modesty's sake. Though to be fair,

Shane wouldn't care. He only had eyes for Shelby. Man, her friend was lucky.

Before she knew it, her eyes had closed and she snuggled under the comforter. She smiled as a vision of Mac, wearing no more than a pair of his own ripped jean shorts, entertained her throughout the night.

And into the morning.

Maggie woke the next day with a pounding headache and a vague sense she needed to be somewhere. On a groan, she rolled onto her back and blinked as a stream of bright sunlight hit her eye. Thankfully, a large body blocked out most of the sun and gave her a moment to focus.

Mac Jameson stared down at her with an intense look on his face.

She blinked up at him. "Shouldn't your shorts be ripped?" Still not sure if she was awake or asleep, Maggie grazed Mac's thigh and felt cotton under her hands. "Sweatpants? What happened to the jean shorts?"

Mac's lips curled into a grin. "Jean shorts? This sounds good."

Maggie realized the dream had come and gone. This Mac was real.

Quickly sitting up, she made sure to keep the cover over her lower half.

His gaze lowered to her chest, and his smile widened. "I really missed a party, didn't I? Saw a wine bottle and drink mix in the kitchen. The clean police are still sound asleep, and there's a gorgeous blond in my room."

"Um, your room?"

He licked his lips and returned his gaze to hers. When she saw the heat melting the blue ice of his eyes, she froze. "Yeah.

20

When I visit, I get the guest room."

"In Shane's house maybe. But this is Shelby's." The pair had decided to keep separate residences until they made the big move to share a home. Maggie figured they'd eventually move into Shane's house because he had more space.

"Her house, his house. What's his is mine. Sort of." Mac ran a callused finger over her cheek, and Maggie found it hard to breathe.

His gaze returned to her chest and lingered. "You are really turning me on."

Stupidly, she stared at his crotch, not surprised to see him hard and growing behind the sweats. "Y-you...ah..."

"Yep. Hard as a rock, just like those pretty nipples." Mac's husky voice snapped her out of her daze. He could see her nipples through her tee-shirt because she'd taken off her bra last night.

He returned his gaze to her face and slowly ran his finger down her jaw to her neck and lower. He continued to trail his finger over her collar bone, to the upper swell of her breast, and down. He rested his finger over her nipple for a moment, and she swore butterflies swarmed in her belly and sent a notice to flood her sex. "I can't wait to suck these."

And she wanted him to suck, to tease, to lick.

So much for a life of celibacy.

Behind him, the sun turned brighter and illuminated the poster on the wall. Of Shelby's guest room.

Maggie jerked back and crossed her arms over her chest—what she should have done the second she spotted Mac standing over her. "Wh-what are you doing here?"

He sighed and sat next to her on the bed.

She squeaked, but before she could scoot away, he gripped her leg through the cover.

"Wait. I'm not going to attack you, okay? I need a minute to cool down." His wry look down at his lap brought a rush of heat to her cheeks. "I came by to get a few books I'd lent Shane. He told me to stop by this morning and grab them. I didn't realize he was taking this whole relationship thing to heart though. Shelby has turned him into a new man."

"What does that mean?"

"He's sleeping in. It's ten on a Saturday morning, and Mr. Type A is still in bed." Mac looked mystified. "She must have given it to him good last night." The speculative gaze he settled on Maggie and the bra hanging over the bedpost spoke volumes.

"Cut it out." She reached for the bra but couldn't grab it without him letting go of her leg.

"Let me." He reached and took the bra from the post, sliding his fingers over the silken cups. "So soft and pretty."

She grabbed it from his hand and snuck it under the sheets, feeling both embarrassed and turned on. Confusion battled with lust in her mind, and she didn't know whether to attack him or pray that he leave. Then the time registered.

"Did you say ten o'clock?"

He nodded.

"Oh my God. The gallery!" Maggie shot out of the bed with her bra and grabbed her jeans, ignoring Mac's wolf whistle.

She raced into the bathroom and hurriedly donned her clothing. Running out into the living room, she said a quick goodbye to a grumpy Shelby and laughing Shane in the kitchen. Thankfully Mac remained out of sight.

Ten o'clock, and she had an hour to dress, clean up, and get to work. As she rushed, her body continued to tingle in funny places, refusing to let her forget Mac's touch. Talk about a hell of a start to her weekend.

CHAPTER THREE

A HELL OF A WAY TO START HIS WEEKEND.

Mac heard Shane and Shelby moving in the house and needed to get a handle on his cock. Or better yet, have Maggie get a handle on it. Good Christ, but the woman was a walking wet dream. Seeing her amazing breasts, her nipples straining though that soft cotton tee-shirt, had been heaven and hell in the same breath. Then to watch her shoot from the bed, to see those toned legs and that tight ass set off by lace panties?

Hell. He worked to regulate his body and relax. Sporting a hard-on while he shared breakfast with his buddy and Shelby probably wouldn't get him invited over again anytime soon. But fuck if he'd be able to see Maggie again without remembering her in bed.

Bad enough he saw her every day in those tight workout clothes. But the blond bombshell in a tee-shirt and panties trumped anything she'd worn the entire time he'd known her.

And those thoughts did nothing to help him calm his raging lust.

After internally reviewing his weekend schedule and

recalling the choice words his uncle had tossed his way after hearing from Wilson "The Jerk" Hussman, Mac finally had a hold of his sex drive.

He walked out and met Shane and Shelby in the kitchen. The pair were kissing and laughing, and Mac felt good seeing them. Shelby had looks, gorgeous curves, and hands from heaven. The woman could crush a rock with her strong fingers, but it was her generous heart and soft spot for Shane that had convinced Mac she was just what Shane needed.

"Cut it out," Mac complained. "Or was I invited over for a show? I came for the eggs, but I'll stay for the entertainment."

"Shut up." Shane flipped him off and laughingly disengaged from his girlfriend.

"I saw Maggie."

Shelby smiled like a cat considering a bowl of cream. "Did you now?"

"Yep. Freaked her the hell out too. She darted out of the house like her hair was on fire."

Shelby blinked and checked the time on the clock. "Oh boy. She'll be lucky to make it to work on time. Too many margaritas last night."

"She never talks about the gallery." A perfect opening, Mac thought, to pump Shelby for information. "She's an artist, right? What does she do, exactly?"

Shelby left the kitchen and returned moments later with a framed piece of art she handed him. "She makes paper."

"Uh, what?" He stared at the piece, intrigued by the patterns and variation of texture and color. It was kind of pretty, in an artsy kind of way.

"Paper. Not the kind you write on, dumb ass," Shane answered. "It's art. Paper is her medium."

"Right, Mr. High Brow." He shook his head and handed

the frame back to Shelby. "Since when are you so into art?"

"Since Shelby made me see what Maggie does. It's pretty cool, actually. She has a paper press and inks. Dyes her stuff and creates real art. She also does some amazing watercolors. I didn't realize she was into all that stuff. I've only seen her prancing around in tights at the gym."

Shelby glared at him. "Shane."

"Sorry. It's his bad influence." He pointed to Mac.

"True." Mac grinned, smiling wider when Shelby sighed. "So why do you suppose Maggie won't give me the time of day? She comes in to work, does her job, and leaves. I'm lucky if I get a frown half the time."

Shelby looked uncomfortable.

"Come on. I'm not going to hurt her. I just want a date. That's it." He had to get this craving for the woman out of his mind.

"Please." Shane snorted. "Like that's all you want."

"Shut up, dickhead." If Shane ruined his shot at Maggie, Mac would clock him. He turned back to Shelby and put on his most charming expression. "Look, I know what you probably think of me. But I'm not as bad as Shane would have you believe."

"He's worse," Shane muttered.

"I've dated a lot of women, I admit. But I was open. I never cheated on any of them. I can't help it if I haven't met the right woman yet. I mean, you think it's hard weeding through the losers? Try being a guy. I'm expected to hold the door, but if I do, some woman yells at me for being a chauvinist. I compliment a woman on her looks, and I'm supposedly leering. When I don't look at her breasts, I'm gay."

Shane choked on the sip of coffee he'd just taken. "Who called you gay?"

"Hetty Leeson."

Shane laughed. "That woman is seventy years old."

"And pissed I won't take out her granddaughter." To Shelby, he explained, "Hetty lives next door to my uncle. She's constantly on me to go out with her granddaughter."

"In Mac's defense, Anna Leeson looks like she was hit with the ugly stick. A lot."

Shelby bit her lip. "That's not nice, Shane."

Mac added, "She's too skinny, and her attitude could use some work. Woman is a bi—ah, a witch. She's constantly on my uncle about his dog, and the damn thing barely barks or moves. In dog years, Buster is the same age as my uncle. Like Uncle Ian's really going to get rid of it because Hetty doesn't like pets? He's had the dog for eight years."

"Oh. Well then." Shelby nodded. "Don't go out with the granddaughter."

"Right." Mac had her. "I should find someone nicer. Someone caring and kind who values the same things I do. A healthy lifestyle. Eating right. Safe sex, or in Maggie's case, no sex."

Shelby frowned. "What?"

Mac ignored Shane frantically shaking his head behind her. "I'm not having sex either. A clean slate, you could call it. I figured it's time I stopped messing around and tried to find someone real." *To screw like no tomorrow.* "I mean, you two seem happy. So I figured I'd cut out the unnecessary sex and focus on just one woman. If she'll give me a chance." Total bullshit, because who the hell thought sex was unnecessary? But he'd told the truth about not getting any. Ever since he'd first seen Maggie, he didn't want anyone else. The woman seriously screwed with his love life. In a bad way. He figured the sooner he had her, the sooner he could move on.

Shane slumped.

Shelby turned on him. "You told him about Maggie? That was said in confidence."

"Sorry, honey. I forgot."

Mac did his best not to laugh. "I'm not going to say anything. Hell, Shelby. Who am I gonna tell? It's not like I'm getting any action either."

"Yeah, right." She didn't look like she believed him. *Shit.*

Shane spoke up, still glaring at Mac. "Actually, that's true. The guy hasn't been with a woman in months, far as I can tell. Not that I keep tabs on him, but he seems to be fixated on Maggie."

"I wouldn't say fixated on her. I just like her. What's so wrong about her and me going on a date?" He couldn't eat, sleep, or work without thinking about Maggie Doran. Time he found out what it was about her that messed with his mind so he could get her out of his system. But he'd do it the right way. They'd date like real people, have some mind-blowing sex, then move on. No mess, no fuss. And he could breathe again without wondering what the petite blond was up to all the time.

"You can't screw around with her," Shelby warned. She put her hands on her hips and stared him down like the Amazon Shane often compared her to. "She's a nice person."

"I know that. Hell, *I'm* a nice person. Why do you assume she'll be the one hurt if we go out? Maybe she'll break *my* heart." He turned to Shane. "What the hell have you been telling her about me?"

"Other than the truth?" Shane shrugged. "Personally, I think you and Maggie would make a great couple. But no way in hell am I playing cupid."

Shelby glared at him before turning back to Mac, "I like you, Jameson. I'll help you. But I'm warning you. You hurt her,

I'll rip your knee off and shove it up your ass."

Impressed, Mac grinned. "Is that the therapist or Maggie's best friend talking?"

"Both. Deal with it."

"No problem. Now how do I get Maggie to go out with me?"

"With that woman? You don't give her a chance to say no."

Nine hours later, Mac waited in Maggie's apartment, grateful Shelby had taken pity on him and let him inside. He'd worked on appearing pathetic for days, had practiced what he'd say to get Shelby's help, and despite Shane's advice to find another way to get to Maggie, he'd scored.

Now he just had to work the magic that had successfully won over the hearts and bodies of the many women he'd dated. Problem was, he'd been trying for months with Maggie, and she didn't seem to appreciate his charm.

He resolved to take a few of Shelby's hints to heart. Maggie liked a dominant personality. All her exes had been dicks. They either treated her like crap or were too weak to handle her. Maggie might be pint-sized—she came up the middle of his chest—but the woman had balls bigger than most men he knew. He wondered if he could push her boundaries in the bedroom.

Most of the woman he'd slept with hadn't been into the rougher stuff. And not wanting to scare any of them, he held himself back when he'd sensed their limits. But Maggie was different. Would she like him taking charge in bed? Being tied up, fucked hard, ordered around?

One could only hope.

With a sigh, he told himself to take things one step at a

time. First, build some trust. No fucking until he'd gotten to know her better and showed her she could depend on him. She knew him from the gym, so he hoped she had some idea he wasn't a complete prick. Well, not all the time.

He stood up from the small loveseat he'd been sitting on and absorbed the feel of her place, taken with her vivid colors and artistic expression. Her small apartment suited her. Located in Queen Anne just a few blocks from the gallery where she worked, the small two bedroom unit was a gem, an old Victorian converted into two apartments. Maggie had the left half of the home, which boasted a cozy fireplace and old hardwood floors. In the living room, she'd positioned a loveseat and reading chair to face a television too small to be considered a distraction. Magazines and romance novels filled her built-in bookcase in the living room. Behind the couch, she'd fashioned a dining room with an antique table and four chairs. Tiny but cozy.

She didn't have a lot of knickknacks, but the artwork on her walls livened the place. He wasn't an artsy guy, but he liked her taste in decorating. Another plus to the woman.

He walked down the hallway leading past a powder room and into the larger of the two bedrooms. Her bedroom smelled like lavender and looked like a bomb had hit it. Her bed was unmade and clothes and shoes covered the floor. He grinned, realizing she must have been frantic to get to work on time. Mac spotted her lace bra on the floor and shuddered. He *really* wanted to see her in that, and soon.

He refrained from going through her closet and drawers, not wanting to be a creepy stalker-type. As it was, he'd have to do some fancy talking to convince her not to freak out and call the cops on him when she returned. But since Shelby had let him in, he figured he had an edge on the law.

He wandered into the kitchen, pleased to see she kept this room neat as a pin. No dirty dishes or food littered the counters. The small area stood apart from the living room by a narrow counter that had stools under it on the living room side. The open design gave the space an inviting grandness. That and the sunny butter color on the walls.

In the fridge, he found fruits and veggies but no meat. He frowned, not recalling whether she ate meat or not. Seattle was filled with health nuts. Though he worked out like a mad man, he didn't live his life like a monk. He enjoyed a good steak now and then. He found himself wondering what it would be like to sit across the table with Maggie and enjoy dinner.

For some odd reason, he had bizarre fantasies of just being with her. Nothing sexual, but domestic shit. Like holding hands and taking walks. Going to movies or sitting around, talking. If he'd told Shane any of this, his friend would fall over laughing. Mac didn't do serious relationships. He'd seen too many of them crumble, his parents a prime example. His uncle, the closest thing he had to a real father, had been taken to the cleaners by a greedy witch who didn't know how to keep her legs closed. No, Mac didn't do relationships. He fucked, he had fun, and he moved on.

He left the kitchen and looked around her dining room, lost in thought. Why the hell did Maggie intrigue him so much? He'd been rejected by women before. Granted, not many said no to him, but he normally accepted refusals with little care. Maggie bugged the shit out of him.

The rattle of keys and a feminine curse alerted him that it was do-or-die time. The doorknob turned and then the door opened.

Maggie entered wearing a slender black skirt that hit her at the knee. Black pumps accentuated her small feet and made her calves that much sexier. A wool coat covered her upper body until she shrugged out of it, revealing another of those body-hugging sweaters that kept him up at night. Jesus, Maggie had a rack worth dying over.

She hung up her jacket and took two steps in his direction before lifting her head.

The moment she saw him she screamed and stopped dead in her tracks. She slapped her hand over her heart, breathing hard, and stared at him.

"Damn. Sorry. Shelby let me in." Mac made sure to keeps his hands in his jeans pockets. No need to startle her further or make himself look threatening. He leaned back against the dining table and tried to look smaller. "So how are you?"

"Y-you… What the *hell* are you doing here?" She took a few deep breaths and let them out before moving toward him.

Relieved she wasn't scared of him, he shrugged. "I figured it was time we talked."

"Talked," she parroted. "About what? I just saw you eight hours ago."

"Nine hours ago."

"What do we have to talk about now?"

"Why won't you go out with me?" he asked boldly.

She blinked. "Huh?"

Not the response he'd been hoping for. "I want to go out with you. On a date."

"You want to have sex with me."

"Well, that too. But I'd like to get to know you first." He grinned, but she didn't smile.

Her eyes narrowed. "Let's lay it all out. You've been wanting to get me naked since day one."

"Okay. Yeah."

"You don't deny it?"

"Why should I? You're smokin' hot. I've seen you for four straight months in nothing but tights and sports bras. Hell yeah, I want a shot at your body." Why the hell did women have to make things difficult? He'd asked her out, flat out told her he wanted to know her better. And now he told the truth about wanting her. Shouldn't she be flattered by his attention?

"That's what I thought." She sighed.

They stared at each other in silence, before he said, "You look tired."

"Yeah? Well I had too many drinks last night, was forced to watch Avatar for the millionth time, and then woke up to you leering at me. I was also two seconds from being late to work. Now all I want to is to get in my comfy clothes and relax."

She looked so worn down, and so damn cute. Mac's heart felt funny, but he ignored it. Had to be the lust making him feel so weird around her all the time.

"Should I apologize for barging in?"

"Whatever." She walked out of her heels and put herself another two inches shorter than him.

"Don't hit me."

"Why?"

Mac closed the distance between them and dragged her into his arms.

"*Mac.*"

Finally. She said his name. He hugged her tight, taking comfort in the feel and scent of her. Her hair smiled like wildflowers, and he had the insane thought he was hugging a fairy—a stacked fairy that could easily have starred in her own adult movies. "You looked like you needed this."

She remained stiff for a moment, then eased into his embrace. Like a puppy wriggling to get more comfortable, she moved until her curves fit against the hard plane of chest. Just right.

"You are so bossy. And so warm," she murmured.

He stroked her hair, amused and freaked out about this odd hug. Especially since he'd initiated it. "You have to do me a favor. Promise not to tell Shelby or Shane about this. A freakin' hug. We should be rolling naked on the floor together by now."

She laughed softly, and he ran his hands from her hair to her back, smoothing over her tense muscles. "I never agreed to have sex with you."

"You should. Sex is a great stress reliever."

"Yeah, well, according to the ladies at the gym, you would know."

Oh hell. Maggie hadn't meant to let that slip.

He pulled back to look at her, and damn him, but his eyes looked impossibly blue. "Don't tell me *you* listen to the rumors at the gym?"

She blushed but didn't turn away. "I can't help it. Jameson's Gym is like its own tiny universe. It's hard not to hear that the great stud at the gym has slept with just about all the female members."

Instead of being put in his place, Mac grinned. "Not Mrs. Hicks. I mean, I could have had her, but I didn't want to piss off my uncle."

Maggie couldn't help her laugh. "Better not let him hear you say that. He's way too young for her. Ida Hicks is ninety years old. Okay, so she's the one woman you haven't had sex with."

"Please. There are a ton of women I've never been with." He paused. "There's you."

A quiet settled between them, one that made her nervous…and aroused. The man got to her on every level. It just figured she'd been thinking about him all day and her traitor of a best friend had let him into her house.

"Right. There's me." She cleared her throat and tried to move away, but he wouldn't let her. "Um, Mac? Let me go."

"Since you said my name, okay." He released her and stepped back looking smug.

This Mac Jameson she knew too well. "I say your name all the time."

"When you're not calling me a jerk, a dictator, or an asshole, you usually call me Jameson." He crossed those incredible arms over his massive chest.

She refrained from fanning herself and planted her hands on her hips, wanting to appear strong, not swoony from the sight of his incredible body. "You *are* a jerk, a dictator and an asshole. Sometimes."

"You're just as bossy. You're just prettier about it." He grinned, and the flash of that smile melted her resolve to keep her distance. "For the record, I think I slept with maybe three women who work out at the gym, and the last one was months ago. Not my fault they have big mouths."

A surge of jealousy struck her mute. Totally not how she wanted to feel about her *boss*. She cleared her throat. "Right. Let's get back on track."

"Oh, let's."

"Shelby let you into my apartment. You want to have sex with me, and you want to talk."

"I want a date."

That surprised her. "Why? If I agree to take off my clothes and let you screw me right now, will that end your pursuit? I mean, we both know what you really want, right?"

He blinked as he digested her words, and she had the satisfaction of knowing she'd thrown him for a loop.

In a low growl, he asked, "So you'd fuck me right here, right now, to get me off your case?"

"Sure. Why not?" God, she would. She really would. She'd been dancing around her attraction for four long months. She trusted Mac, well, not as a boyfriend, but as a man who would never force her or physically hurt her.

Not unless she wanted him to.

And there went another pair of panties.

"Damn." He scrubbed his hair and took a surprising step back. "Tell you what. Go get comfortable and we'll have that talk."

Not what she'd expected to hear. "Excuse me?"

His familiar arrogance returned. "Did I stutter? Go put your hot little ass in comfortable clothes and get back here."

She wished his bossiness didn't arouse her so much. She grumbled as she walked away. "I'll change because *I* want to change, not because you're telling me what to do. It's my freakin' house."

She heard him mutter something about annoying women but had a hard time getting over the fact that he liked the way she looked. He always called her hot or pretty or beautiful, words she'd been hearing her entire life. But when he said it, she actually believed it.

She returned moments later in clean panties, her favorite flannel pants, her comfy bra, a sweatshirt, and her fuzzy socks. Her relaxing and totally unappealing clothes. A pitiful defense, but if she felt unattractive, she prayed she could stop herself from jumping the man.

Maggie didn't want to be another notch on his bedpost. And right now, aroused and excited, she feared she'd look without leaping. The notion of having an orgasm with Mac—no longer *Jameson*—had indeed become an obsession.

"Well? I'm here. Talk." She glared at Mac sitting on her loveseat. He'd started a fire, and the place looked way too cozy not to get closer.

He patted the spot next to him. "Sit by me."

She snorted. "My house. My rules." She deliberately took a seat in the chair opposite the loveseat.

He sighed, rose to his formidable height, and crossed the room to loom over her.

"Did I stutter?" she mocked, repeating him from earlier.

He lifted her into his arms in one fell swoop.

"*Mac.*"

"You weigh a lot more than you look." He laughed at her, then sat with her on the loveseat before dumping her next to him.

When she scrambled to back away and off the loveseat, he took her foot in his hand. "Uh-uh. Sit. Stay."

"I'm not a damn dog," she snapped.

"You know, you saying that just makes me want to collar you."

She froze. Collar? Had he looked through her private journals?

"I was just kidding, Maggie." Mac chuckled. "I can just imagine a collar and leash on you. Kinky, but I doubt you'd go for that." He winked at her.

If the man only knew how often she'd imagined being dominated.

"Look, I just want to talk," he continued.

"Yeah, right."

He squeezed her foot, and to her surprise, it felt good. "Do that again."

"If I rub your feet, will you shut up and listen?"

She moaned when he started massaging her arches. "Man, that's good. Okay, you can talk."

He coughed and shifted under her. "Much as I look forward to you making those sounds when I'm coming inside you, I kind of wanted to say something first."

She jerked her foot back. "*What?*"

He pulled it back. Then he rubbed her toes and she forgot to be angry. "Talk, Jameson."

"No. Mac. Say, talk, *Mac*."

"Keep rubbing my feet and I'll call you whatever you like."

He chuckled. "Good to know." He soothed her tired pads and hit her heels hard. The man was a wonder. "Look. This is awkward. You work for me. Only because you want to, I know. We've known each other for months. Your best friend is dating my best friend, and you're probably freaked out that if you fall in love with me, you'll make things awkward when we get together for parties and shit."

"Excuse me?"

"I want you. You want me. We're two attractive people. Why shouldn't we hit it?"

She wanted to laugh. This was the Mac she knew. Honest. Sometimes to a fault. It made her feel better that he didn't try to soften her up or seduce her with lies. "Everything you said makes sense. If we did go out and it turned sour, maybe because *you* fell in love with *me*, and I left your sorry ass behind, it would make it tough to hang out with Shane and Shelby. Though we don't do that much with them together as it is."

"Only because you go out of your way to avoid me."

There was that. "I'm busy. I'm working two jobs, you know."

"I don't know. You never talk to me. Tell me about your

art stuff."

She took a hard look at him. He seemed so earnest. "Why?"

"Because I'd like to know more than that I'm fucking the hot blond from the gym. I want a date, Maggie. Wherever we go from there will be up to you."

Astonished, she sat up straighter. "Hold on. You think you can get me into bed after one date?"

He grinned. "Honey, I could have your ankles on my shoulders in about three seconds if I tried. Let's not embarrass you. I'm a sexy guy. I know it, you know it. I'm trying to be a gentleman."

"You aren't serious?" She drew her foot back, aware he let her. "Think pretty highly of yourself, don't you?" Yet that was part of his charm. Mac was handsome, and he knew it. He treated all women with politeness and charm—except for her, it seemed. Those lucky few who received his *special* attention had nothing but good things to say about him.

"Think?" Mac snorted. "I *know* I'm damn good. Let me show you what you've been missing."

And then the conceited hunk did what she'd been dreaming about for months.

He kissed her.

CHAPTER FOUR

MAGGIE DIDN'T HAVE TIME TO CATCH HER BREATH before Mac was on top of her, pressing her down into the cushions. He caged her with his strong arms, but he also put space between their bodies, bearing down with his mouth more than his frame.

She wasn't penned in. If she wanted to break the kiss, she could. Not that she wanted to. Maggie concentrated on the drugging warmth of his mouth.

He tasted sweet, as if he'd had something minty. His mouth was firm, his tongue bold. Mac didn't ask, he took. The kiss had her losing her will to resist in seconds. And the bastard no doubt knew it.

This was what she'd feared. Their instant, physical attraction couldn't be denied, not after this. She'd never been so in tune with a man, or so in lust. He moaned and deepened the kiss while keeping himself apart, not touching her with anything more than his mouth.

Unable to resist, she reached up and pulled him down, wanting to feel him on top of her. She ran her hands over his thick neck and dense chest. All that muscle, so strong. And all hers.

"Fuck, yeah. Touch me," he whispered as he kissed his way down her jaw to her throat. He nipped under her ear while she eased her hands under his shirt. The feel of his corded abs contracting under her fingers intrigued her. Mac might be king of the mountain, but she had queenly skills. She pinched his nipples and scratched her nails over his chest.

His immediate reaction gratified. He let out a curse and slammed his mouth on hers again. Eating her up, sucking her desire to the forefront until nothing mattered but getting him inside her.

And then he stopped. Stone cold still.

He rested his forehead against hers, breathing hard.

"Mac?"

"Shh. Hold on." He took big gulping breaths. "I'm two seconds away from fucking you raw. And I told you. I want a date first."

She tried to make sense of him. "So you don't want to have sex." Had she ever been turned down at this stage of play? A few old boyfriends had used her to get off. But they'd rejected her after the fact. Never in the *middle* of having sex.

"What? No. Yes." He swore again and lifted his head to stare down at her. "Your eyes are so damn pretty." His gaze lowered to her mouth. "You have no idea how badly I want to see you swallow my cock. I want to shove hard up that pussy and come deep inside you."

Oh man. Now they were talking.

"But I want that date first."

She didn't get it.

"Oh hell. I'm screwing this up." He sat back, leaving her aching and tired and frustrated. "I want you. But I don't want to just fuck and fly. I want us to get to know each other better."

"You do?"

"I like you, okay?" he snapped. Then his gaze caught on her mouth again. "*Hell.*" He kissed her and didn't stop there. No longer content to just touch her with his mouth, he put those big hands everywhere. Her shoulders, her arms, her breasts. He seemed fascinated with her chest as he kissed her.

Before she knew it, he had her straddling him on the loveseat while he kissed and fondled her into near-orgasm.

"I want to see you come," he growled as he nipped his way down her throat. He lifted her ratty sweatshirt and sucked her nipples right through her bra. At the same time, he shoved his hand under the waist of her panties, seeking the heat of her. His fingers slid over her slick clit and continued into her pussy. "You're so wet. So tight." He groaned and kissed her.

Maggie didn't know what to think. One minute she'd been having near sex, then he pulled back. Now he was sticking his fingers inside her and bringing her quickly to climax.

He shoved his tongue in her mouth and echoed the penetration with his fingers. Hard and fast, he plunged them inside her while grazing her taut clit. Then he broke the kiss to nip her neck and shoved his fingers deeper.

Between one breath and the next, she exploded.

"Yeah, give it to me," she dimly heard him say as she clenched around him.

God, it had been so long, and it had never, *ever*, been like this. He felt so good. Hard and tough beneath her. He resumed kissing her neck then found her mouth again.

She kissed him back, thanking him without words.

When he withdrew his fingers, she felt the loss. And she realized the full import of what she'd just done and with whom. Notch number three hundred and four on Mac's bedpost.

Damn it.

"You came hard for me." His satisfaction was hard to miss, as was the bulge still solid beneath his jeans. "Now we're going to have our date."

"Tonight?" she asked stupidly. He'd had her. Kind of. What was his fixation on a date? Or was that some kind of code for convincing her to get him off?

"Not tonight. You had a long day. You're tired." He kissed her, and she felt exhausted all of a sudden.

"But you didn't..."

"Nope. I'm saving that for you."

"I didn't agree to have sex with you." She felt like an idiot for saying that considering he'd just fingered her to orgasm. But still, his arrogance grated.

Especially when he raised a brow and just looked at her.

"You shouldn't assume," she persisted.

He smiled, and the approval in his gaze warmed her. "That's why I like you. Even when you look so soft and tired, you're a ball buster." He fitted her limp hand over his crotch, where she felt a very large, solid erection. "You're going to take care of this for me at some point."

"After our date," she said and squeezed him. "*If* we have one."

He closed his eyes, as if in pain. When he opened them, the need blazing there stole her breath. "After our date."

She fought for control of herself and sat up straight, still straddling him. She removed her hand and righted her clothing, all while the powerful male remained tense under her. "If it will get you to stop begging," she said with a sigh, "I guess I'll agree to go out with you. Pathetic, Jameson."

He grinned, but the mean glint in his eye told her not to underestimate him. The man turned her on without even trying.

So unfair. "You know I'm going to make you pay for that."

"You can try." She blew him a kiss. "But after tonight, it's going to be hell for you, thinking that you had those fingers inside me. Every time you see me, you'll know what it was like to suck my nipple and kiss my mouth." *Yes.* Finally, sexy Maggie came to the fore with a man. Not shy, submissive, doormat Maggie.

His chest heaved with her every word. "You're a cruel woman. I really, *really* like that." He kissed her hard on the mouth and pulled her hips close to grind over his arousal. "I can't wait for our date." He set her aside and stood, then pulled her to her feet. "Walk me out."

"Quit bossing me around." She never would have imagined she'd like this side of Mac. She still didn't understand why he'd let her come but hadn't gotten off. Or why he persisted in this date nonsense. "You do realize we'll never be a couple, right? We should just have sex and end this before it gets started."

He paused at her front door. "Oh?"

"You're Mr. Macho. I'm a strong, independent woman. You have money. Yeah, I've seen your car. Don't pretend. I'm the starving artist type. You also can't commit to women, and despite what tonight might have been about, I'm not into one-night stands."

"I know." He brushed her hair back from her face. So gentle, those hands that only a week ago had been wrapped around a man's throat. "I also know you're going through a dry spell. I'm happy to help you through it."

"A—*what?*" Had Shelby told him about her new celibate lifestyle? How embarrassing. *I'm going to kill that mouthy brunette.*

"Don't worry about it. I like knowing you've been saving yourself for me."

"Cocky bastard." Over his laughter, she added, "I'll have you know I could have a man at the snap of my fingers. Wilson, Brent…even you."

His laughter faded. "You snap those fingers at anyone but me and we'll have some problems."

That dominance turned her on. But she couldn't be an independent woman and like that kind of attitude in a man, could she? "Who the hell are you to tell me what to do?"

He shook his head. "I thought we weren't going to play games. I'm the guy who just made you come all over his fingers. I'm the guy you're going out with tomorrow night."

"A Sunday night date?" She intentionally ignored the part about climaxing. Oh man, had she.

He waited.

Maggie wanted to be alarmed. She should have been ranting and raving over his attitude. Who the hell did he think he was? But as she watched him watching her, she knew a sense of excitement. Why not see where this might take them? Some harmless fun. And if he could make good on his promises of domination and control, she would more than take him up on his offer.

"So you think you're man enough to control me, huh?"

"Yeah, I do. We agreed to a date. We're eventually gonna fuck. Because that's inevitable. We click. Admit it."

"Sure. Physically, we seem to hit it off. But that doesn't mean—"

"And you like me bossing you around. If you didn't, you'd have quit by now. Besides, if you really listened to the rumors at the gym, you know I like being in charge."

She'd heard that. Nothing specific, but the innuendo that Mac tended to get domineering in bed. No wonder he had women dying to get their claws into him. With his looks, money, and power, he was a dream come true. Except that part where he never lost the attitude and went through women like the flavor of the day.

"Whatever, Jameson."

He just shook his head. "We're having that date tomorrow night. And after that, well, don't say I didn't warn you."

"Wait. Warn me about what?"

He turned to the door. She grabbed his arm, that thick, powerful forearm, and he stopped.

"Yes?" he drawled with excessive patience.

"You want a date, fine. But we can't let this get weird. There's Shane and Shelby. And I work for you."

"Technically you work for my uncle. He owns the gym. I just run it." He covered her hand with his. "This isn't weird. It's called going out. Normal people do it all the time."

"Normal people? I just had an orgasm on my loveseat," Maggie had to mention. *Holy shit.* She'd had an orgasm. Her first in over a year not instigated by her own hand. A miracle.

"True. I'm thinking you owe me one." He leaned close to kiss her. "Dress casual. You're coming to my place for dinner tomorrow. I'll pick you up at six. And don't forget your class tomorrow at two. Nicole said you'd cover for her."

He left before she could argue.

Not that she had anything left to add. She'd agreed to cover for Nicole's step class tomorrow. And she had nothing better to do on a Sunday night than read a book and wash her hair. Sad but true.

Maggie cleaned up and went to bed, not sure tonight had actually happened. Had Mac really been waiting in her apartment? Had the man truly made her come with no more than a few kisses and some very heavy petting?

Just thinking about what he'd done to her made her hot

and bothered, as did the remembrance of how big and solid his cock had felt. Thoughts of having that inside her brought forth all the naughty fantasies she'd harbored. But how would Mac feel about fulfilling them? It would be really embarrassing to open up to him—Shane's best friend—if he thought her some kind of crazy pervert.

She'd had a few boyfriends who tried to be more controlling for her, but she hadn't bought the act. In the end, the sex had been a letdown, the relationship fizzling soon after. What few jerks she didn't confide in had been wrong for her from the beginning.

For some reason, Maggie wanted to be controlled in the bedroom. She'd had fantasies about it for years, and the one time an ex-boyfriend had been close to getting it right, she'd been halfway to heaven in love, then found out he had a girlfriend on the side. Unfortunately, most of the men she sought to give her that submissive feeling acted like pricks. Mac was the first guy she'd met who seemed somewhat normal. Controlling, yes, but not cruel. Just sure of himself. Okay, the man acted conceited. She'd admit that. But he had a right to be that sexually assured with a body that fine.

What guy had she been with in the past five years—hell, make that ten years—had made her come so easily, then left without getting his? She still didn't know what to make of that, or his odd request for a date.

Did the king of no commitment want a relationship? Maybe he looked to Shane and Shelby as inspiration. Did he want Maggie to be his girlfriend? Because that kind of close tie freaked her out. She'd never made good choices with men, and Maggie actually liked Mac. She didn't want to screw up a good thing. To her way of thinking, they could have sex, remain friends, and see each other socially when with their best buds.

Group outings without all the drama and angst that accompanied her failed relationships.

And after the sex, they could and would remain casual friends. Friends with benefits. She could do that. So she hoped.

The next night she sat shuffling through the cable stations when a knock sounded at the door. A glance at the clock made her sigh. Mr. Marine, a good ten minutes early. Go figure.

"I'm not dressed yet," she yelled out.

"Then I'm definitely coming in."

She laughed to herself and crossed to the door. She opened it, and Mac pushed past her inside. "Grab your jacket. Let's go."

"Hello. And how are you today? I'm fine. What? Yes. The class went well. The gym wasn't too crowded."

He snorted. "Yeah, yeah. How are you? Good to hear. You look stunning, as usual. And no, I haven't slept with anyone between last night, when you left me hard and frustrated, and now."

She blinked at him as she grabbed her jacket. "I don't think I asked about your sex life."

"You should. Responsible partners are all about safe sex."

"Oh my God. Are you lecturing me?"

The fifteen minute drive to his house grew into a debate about sexual responsibility. As usual, the argument was more about needling Mac than being right. Half the time she said things just to annoy him.

"Oh yeah. For me, a condom is a *must*," she emphasized.

He frowned. "But you said you're on birth control."

"Duh, because I'm not ready for kids yet. But birth control doesn't prevent disease."

"Um, I get that. But I told you I'm clean," he said as he

parked the car.

She left the vehicle with him and walked up the drive. "I thought we were talking in generalities. Why the push to have sex with me? I thought this was just a date. You know. Where we *talk* to each other."

He ground his teeth and let her into the house. "For such a small person, you have a big mouth."

"I'm not that small. Unless I stand next to freakishly large people, like yourself."

"You mean, freakishly *sexy* people. I know I make you uncomfortable, being so hot and godlike. It's okay, Maggie. I'll take good care of you."

She shoved him out of the way and took a good look at his place. "I'm amazed your ego fits through the door."

The large home in Green Lake fit what she'd imagined his finances to be. According to Shelby, who'd heard it from Shane, Mac had made a bunch of great investments over the years, diversifying. So unlike many in this economy, he actually had money to fall back on, added to his military retirement. He drove a new car that had to cost a pretty penny. And his home boasted hardwood floors, leather furniture, and exquisite built-in cabinetry around a stone fireplace. A few black and white photographs of different countries and places graced the walls. He didn't have a lot of clutter, but he had pictures and Marine Corps mementos filling up a wall unit to the left of the fireplace.

She saw him in the décor, but she also thought he'd had help. "This is way too neat for you. I was expecting black leather and chrome. Some nudie posters and pizza boxes." She liked that he narrowed his eyes, obviously irked. "So who helped you decorate?"

"Why is it so hard to believe I did it myself?"

She just stared at him.

He blew out a breath. "Fine. Shane's mom helped me stage the stuff. But it was my taste. I picked out the furniture."

"Hmm." She ran a hand over the back of the leather sectional. "Feels nice, and it's big enough for that monstrously large body of yours."

"And my ego. Don't forget how big that is," he said sarcastically.

"There is that." She waited for it.

"It goes without saying, I'm big all over."

"I knew you wouldn't let that one slide."

He chuckled. "See? You do know me. Isn't it nice, being all friendly?"

She shook her head and moved deeper into the house. Through a nice dining room big enough to seat six, she entered a gourmet kitchen. Jealous, because she'd always wanted something so nice, she took in the stainless steel appliances, black granite counter tops and top of the line pots hanging from a pot rack above the center island. He even had a prep sink in which a colander of fresh veggies sat.

"Don't tell me you cook."

"Why ruin your already sterling opinion of me?" He stepped around her and moved to the main sink, where he rolled up the sleeves of his dark blue sweater and washed his hands.

As usual, she had a hard time looking away. The sight of his strong forearms and large hands enthralled her. Mac didn't play at being strong. He *was* strong. More than physically, he had a warrior's spirit, an indomitable will to take charge and maintain order, and it never failed to fill her daydreams with just what he might be like in bed. Or worse, as a boyfriend.

She blinked as he finished wiping his hands on a towel.

"Penny for your thoughts."

"Please. Mine cost a lot more than that."

He chuckled and moved to the vegetables, then set to chopping them up with military precision.

"So you really cook?"

"Yep. I learned the hard way. Cook or starve. I chose to learn some culinary skills."

"Ouch."

"Yeah, well, my uncle can barely boil water. I'm usually fixing stuff for him."

"I like Ian." She mentally compared him to Mac. "You look alike. He's just as big and mouthy as you are."

"Thanks." Mac reached for a pan, grabbed a bottle of olive oil from above, and set everything over the burner. From the fridge, he removed a tray of steak and onions. He added that and a small bowl of seasoning and started frying up their dinner.

"You look like a pro."

"I'm good. Just ask around." He winked at her.

"Funny, but your uncle was saying the exact same thing to some woman at the gym when I saw him. If I recall, she turned away in a huff while he laughed himself silly."

Mac frowned. "And he has the nerve to tell me to go easy on the members."

"Did you get into trouble because of that incident with Wilson?" For which she'd never thanked him.

"Nah. Uncle Ian was pissed about it until I told him why I choked the guy. Then he understood. We refunded Wilson's money and kicked his ass out of the gym."

"What did you say, exactly?"

"That Wilson had his hand on you and you didn't like it. That was enough for Ian. My uncle taught me a lot growing up, and not hurting women was at the top of his list. Call him a throwback if you want, but I agree with him."

"No, no. I like that. You're gruff and you curse a lot. And let's face it, you're huge. But I've never been scared of you, that you'd hurt me, I mean." She paused. "Thanks for helping me with Wilson."

"You're welcome." For once he didn't act superior. The simple reply was heartfelt and made her rethink what she knew about Mac all over again.

CHAPTER FIVE

"So you keep mentioning your uncle." Maggie wanted to know more. "He raised you, not your parents?"

"My folks split up when I was eight," Mac said matter-of-factly. "My father ended up getting killed by a drunk driver a year later. My mother took off. Haven't seen or heard from her since."

"Ouch."

He grimaced. "Yeah. So Uncle Ian raised me. He was married to a woman he loved like crazy for years. Turned out she was nothing more than a—" He checked himself. "She was fooling around on him and tried to take him for everything he had. A real user."

"No wonder you have issues with women."

He frowned. "I don't have issues. I like women. Hell, I *love* women." He leered at her, but she saw what he hadn't said. The man had trust issues he'd more than earned.

A lot like her. "Well, if it makes you feel better, my folks left me on the doorstep of a church when I was just a baby. Just me and my older brother against the world."

Marie Harte

"No shit?"

"Yep. I'm a blond Little Orphan Annie." She grinned, not bitter at all about how she'd been raised. "Luckily, Trevor and I grew up together in a series of foster homes. We weren't placed with abusive or uncaring people. And we still keep in touch with a few of them."

"Trevor, huh? Does he live close?"

"He travels a lot for work." *Doing secret squirrel stuff for the government his little sister isn't supposed to know about. Corporate shark, my ass. The liar.* "But we're still close, even if we're not physically together. He calls when he can and always brings me stuff from abroad. I don't know if you saw my craft room when you were snooping around my apartment."

"Not snooping. I was waiting for you." He finished with the food and put the pan on a cool burner. After he turned off the stovetop, he fished two plates from a cabinet. "Trust me. I wanted like hell to look through your underwear drawer, but I thought that might freak you out more than just me being there." He put the food on the plates then found a bottle of wine from a built-in wine cooler.

"Man. You have everything in here."

"Just about. Grab a plate."

She did and followed him into the dining room. No candles, but a wine bucket and two place settings complete with wine glasses waited for them. He poured them each a glass.

"Fancy."

"Yeah, because I'm all about appearances." He huffed. "I happen to like wine with my food. But I'd never turn down a good beer. And I don't mean that blue ribbon crap."

"A beer snot. I'm not surprised."

He chuckled. "Like you're not a little snooty yourself. I saw that artwork in your place. Nothing store bought. It's all

54

hand-crafted crap. You didn't have anything commercial in there."

"Well, no. I like what I like."

"Yeah. Me too." The look he shot her was no less than scorching. "So, back to you and your sob story growing up."

Trust Mac to give her no quarter. She liked that about him. When others learned of her humble beginnings, they seemed uncomfortable or even pitying. Not the man still giving her a once-over.

"Your brother," Mac continued. "You and he grew up out here?"

"On the East Coast, actually. We grew up outside of D.C. But we both wanted to move West. It's way too humid out there." She shook her head and took a sip of wine. "Hey, this is good."

"Only the best for you, Maggie." He patted his chest. "Myself included."

She nearly choked on her wine.

"So when did you come out here?"

"You really want to know, or is this just to soften me up for sex later?"

The lazy amusement on his face vanished, to be replaced with real annoyance. "Can't I be curious about you? Why is that wrong? If you don't want to talk, just say so."

"Ah, no." She put her wine down. "Honestly, I'm not used to this. Usually on a date, I sit back and listen while the man of the hour goes on and on about his job and his life. I nod, smile and look pretty."

"You've been dating the wrong guys." He snorted. "Not surprising. You tell me I have trust issues? Check a mirror, honey."

"Look, *sweetcheeks*, I didn't ask for an analysis of my

shortcomings." Irritated with him, she turned back to her plate. He might be an ass, but the smells coming from her dinner made her salivate.

"Easy. I'm not trying to psychoanalyze you. Jesus, just eat, would you? I forgot what a pain in the ass you can be when your blood sugar is low."

How did he know that? She dug into her plate and moaned at the flavors bursting on her tongue.

"Go on. Say it," he demanded.

She wanted to be annoyed, but he'd earned that smug tone.

"It's delicious. This is amazing. Just a few vegetables and steak and it tastes like heaven. How do you cook like this?"

"It's a gift."

"No kidding."

They continued to eat and polished off the bottle of wine. She learned more about him, watching how animated he became when talking about his uncle or Shane. He loved Shane's family as well, particularly Shane's younger brother.

"George idolizes you and you know it," she teased. "He's working hard to become the next Mac Jameson. In the four months I've known him, I've seen him with three different girls."

"Whoa. That's not my style, Maggie." Mac leaned back and grinned. "I'm more the love them and leave them *happy* type."

"I don't know. They seem to be in perpetual mourning at the gym. You have your own set of groupies."

"Yeah? Well you do too." He didn't seem happy about that fact, and his displeasure secretly thrilled her. "Trust me. I've heard more than my share about the hot blond aerobics instructor."

"Lovely."

"Yep. The one with the fine ass and nice tits."

"Mac." She flushed.

"What? Their words, not mine," he protested.

"Yeah, right."

He chuckled. "I mean, I agree with the description, don't get me wrong. But there's more to you than looks, right?" He paused. "You still haven't told me much about your art, and I know that's a big deal. To hear Shelby talk about you, you're the next Van Gogh."

"He was a painter." She paused. "How much do you know about art?"

"Not a thing," he said with pride.

"And you don't seem to care that you know nothing. So sad."

"Hey. I can field strip an M16 in the time it takes you to spell *Van Gogh* backwards. We all have our priorities. Now quit changing the subject. Your art. How'd you get into it?"

She wanted to tell him not to bother buttering her up. She'd mentally agreed to sex with him, despite her prior claims that he not assume they'd eventually come together. But he looked interested. And he'd persisted in trying to talk about *her* tonight. Such a change from the way her dates normally progressed.

She liked his interest and decided to answer him. "I don't know. I always liked creating things. Sculpting especially. Just model clay, nothing fancy. I can draw reasonably well, but it's not something I can make a living doing. For that matter, neither are my current art projects," she ended with a self-deprecating laugh.

"Not to hear Shelby tell it. She said that gallery where you work is selling a lot of your stuff."

"The Beholder is a terrific place. And the new owner

Kim's a gem. She gives me flexible hours at the gallery, so that I can do my art and work for you during my time off."

"I like that. But I still don't get how you got into making paper. I mean, I think paper and I see holes and lines."

"I used to feel the same. Then a few years ago I was bumming around an art gallery in Portland and saw a paper sculpture. The artist happened to be there at the same time, and we started talking."

"Did he invite you to see his etchings?"

"No. *She* showed me her studio and took me on as an apprentice. I helped her prepare and did a lot of cleanup for her. In exchange, she helped me get started. In the garage at my place, I have my own paper press and materials. It's not the best space to work, and it's messy, but it's my own form of expression." She hated that she sounded defensive. A lot of artists looked down on her for her craft, but she loved it. She might not be into oils, watercolors or traditional art, but her medium worked for her.

"Sounds good to me." Mac sat back and nodded. "Like you said, I know nothing about art. But if you made that red picture above your fireplace, I'd say you could more than earn a living selling your stuff."

She brightened. "You liked it?" Then she immediately felt stupid. Of course he'd say what he thought she wanted to hear.

Except he looked uncomfortable. "Yeah. Not that I'm into art or anything, and I don't know that I'd call it pretty, but I couldn't look away from it. The piece had nice detail." He shrugged.

"Shelby bugged the heck out of me to make her something for her birthday. She swears I'm going to be worth big money soon." She sighed. "Maybe after I'm dead. Seems like the curse of most great artists. They're poor until they die." Realizing what she'd said, she corrected herself. "Not that I'm poor. But none of my work goes for millions."

"Not yet." Mac smiled. She saw no censure or taunting there, and she relaxed. "So The Beholder is where you work?" He frowned. "That sounds familiar. Hey, isn't that right down the road from Shelby's clinic?"

"How do you think she and I met? We bumped into each other years ago, and boom. Instant friendship."

"The hot blond and sultry brunette. Fits."

She didn't like hearing him refer to Shelby as sultry. But the fact she felt a hint of jealousy over *her boss* didn't sit well either. She hurried to ignore her weird emotions and pasted a smile on her face. "It's nice to know you think I'm attractive, but you don't need to keep repeating yourself."

"Too used to hearing it, are you? I get that." He gave a put-upon sigh. "Me too. Women are always treating me like a walking billboard for sex. It's tough, being so manly."

"Please."

"No, really." He nodded, but his innocent expression didn't mesh with the devilry in his gaze. "Take my last girlfriend."

"Do you even remember her name?"

He frowned. "Yeah." He paused. "Jessica."

"Jessica what? You don't know, do you?"

He ignored her. "Jessica was all about my body and my wallet. I mean, I was happy to share myself with her, but I was hoping for something more." He looked into her eyes, and the truth there shocked her. Mac wasn't as superficial as she'd once thought. "I didn't expect marriage or anything super serious since we'd just met, but time spent not talking about her boob job and how great she looked would have been nice. The only things she seemed to care about were herself and how much I cleared last year after taxes. Oh, and how much I could bench press." He snorted. "I don't lift weights to look good. I lift because it takes my mind off the fact that I'm *retired*." He sneered the word.

She'd seen the scarring on his left leg and been curious but had never asked. "What happened?"

"Got shot in the knee and it never healed right. So I was medically discharged after two surgeries. Now I do physical therapy, and Shelby's helping. It's not like I could have stayed in the Corps forever anyway." He acted like it was no big deal, but Maggie could tell how much being out of the service bothered him.

"That's where you met Shane, isn't it?" She knew Shane had served in the Marines.

He nodded. "He and I ran into each other a few times when I was active. Then I when I got out two years ago, I ended up seeing him on the street downtown. Weird coincidence. I mean, his folks are just a mile from my uncle. Small world." He smiled.

"Yeah." They quieted and watched each other. Maggie wondered what Mac saw when he looked at her. This was the longest they'd ever talked together, and the majority of the conversation hadn't been about Shane or Shelby.

Mac suddenly stood and cleared their plates.

"I'll wash." She moved to stand, but he barked at her to sit down. "Again. Do I really need to remind you I'm not a dog?"

"You know, there are so many ways I could take this conversation. But I don't want to totally strike out. So I'm gonna put the dishes in the kitchen. You're going to go sit in the living room, and we'll finish up the night—"

"Getting naked?" There. She'd put her cards on the table. She wanted to have sex, so why not take what they both clearly wanted? Except the answer he gave her wasn't what she'd anticipated.

"Watching the new detective movie on TV. And don't even try acting like you don't want to see it. I overheard you the other day talking to Shelby about it."

"You have big ears." So no on the sex, but companionship and an agreement to watch a television movie she'd been looking forward to? The man paid attention to things she liked. How…odd.

She figured out which remote to use and how to use it just as he joined her. Before she could turn the channel, he plucked the remote from her hand and settled her right next to him, hip to hip. His body heat bled through to hers, though she'd have bitten her tongue before telling him how much she liked him sitting so close.

"I am not a doll. You can't just twist me around and bend me ov—"

His laughter made her reconsider what she'd been about to say.

"Oh, shut up and watch the movie, Jameson."

He whispered, "Mac," then nipped her ear.

Her entire body warmed and her nipples hardened. She thought about asking him to skip the movie and move on to the main course—them, in bed. But he pulled his head back and broke the mood. Instead, he cuddled her against his chest and put his arm around her shoulder. The movie started, and they watched together.

Maggie felt comfortable, turned on yet content.

Content. Such a strange feeling to put together with Mac Jameson, but there it was.

The movie droned on, and everything started to blur.

"Maggie, wake up."

She blinked her eyes open to see the credits rolling on the screen. She immediately brushed her mouth.

His laughter vibrated through his broad chest. "Don't worry. No drool. But you do snore a little. It's cute."

"I do not." Her cheeks heated. "So tell me who did it. Was it the CEO's niece or his stepson?"

"I'll never tell."

"Evil man." She scooted out of his embrace and sought the bathroom. She returned moments later to see him standing by the door. He hadn't been kidding about no sex.

Part of her liked him for simply spending the night with her, no strings attached. The other part of her worried he didn't find her to his liking, despite the many times he'd flattered her.

"It's late, and we have work tomorrow."

"Problem with dating your boss is he's all about the schedule." She sighed. "But I am tired."

She gave him another shot to make his move.

When he leaned closer, she felt a moment of relief. Predictable Mac. Her previous notions about the man hadn't been that off the mark.

He placed a kiss on her *cheek* and then moved around her to the closet, where he fetched her jacket. He put it on her while she stared at him in confusion. Wait. He seriously intended to take her home?

"Come on," he growled and dragged her into the bitterly cold night. The drive back to her apartment was over before it had begun, only the sound of classic rock breaking the silence between them. He pulled in front of the old Victorian house and idled the car.

"I guess I'll see you tomorrow," she said, still not quite believing tonight had been so enjoyable or so nonsexual. *Should I invite him in? Is this part of the script?* He didn't appear to be in a hurry to leave the car, yet he'd been adamant thus far to remain casual friends.

"No goodnight kiss?" he teased.

"I thought we did that at your house."

"Please." He huffed. "That peck on the cheek? Woman, I made you dinner. I didn't spoil the ending of the movie, *and* I drove you home without molesting you. That's got to be worth some tongue."

She rolled her eyes. "First you don't want sex, then you do?"

"It's just a kiss." His lips quirked in the moonlight. "Unless you're afraid you won't be able to control yourself."

"Yeah, right. A kiss, you said. Okay, buddy. Pucker up." She unbuckled her seatbelt and slid closer to him. Then she palmed his face, and a spark of desire raced through her at the contact. He closed his eyes, and she closed hers as she leaned closer to kiss him.

Maggie wanted to thank him for being such a gentleman at the same time she wanted to punish him for not making a move. How dare he be so *nice*? All her assumptions about Mac Jameson had gone to the wayside. A womanizer? Maybe, but not a complete jerk. He didn't muscle in on her or try to take advantage.

What the hell?

The kiss started soft until she traced his lips with her tongue. His hands moved to her shoulders, and she scooted closer, angling her mouth over his. She thrust her tongue between his lips, stroking his tongue with hers while she deepened the kiss.

Tingles lit her from her mouth all the way to her core, dampening her panties and making her want much more from the man.

He gripped her jacket and soon took charge of the kiss, drawing on her tongue and nipping at her lips while he intoxicated her with desire.

Mac Jameson would be hell on wheels in the sack…if she could get him there.

The bastard pulled away, panting. His eyes were darker blue, his mouth parted, slick, and sexy as hell.

"*Fuck.* You and I are definitely getting horizontal."

"When?" she rasped, irked to have to follow *his* timetable. Her body screamed at her to straddle his hips slide over that thick shaft, taking it inside her where it would do the most good.

"When?" he moaned. "I'd say right the hell now, but that negates my good behavior all evening."

"Negates? Big word for you, Mac."

He chuckled. "You're looking frustrated, sweetheart."

"Oh?" She unbuckled his seatbelt and gripped the bar in his pants, gratified by his hiss. "What's this, then? A little of your own *frustration* for me?"

"Damn it. Let me go."

But he thrust into her hand. Not the action of a man not interested.

"Why don't we end the night the way we ended last night?"

"What?"

She unbuttoned his fly, all the way down, while keeping her gaze on his. The need on his face exacerbated her arousal, to the extent she almost didn't care that they were in his vehicle…in front of the house.

"Turn off the car."

"Why?" he asked even as he turned the key and shut off the engine and lights.

The silence was broken by his low moan as she reached inside his boxer briefs and found him hard, his slit wet.

"You know why." She leaned close to kiss him again and started pumping him.

He met her more than halfway, wrapping his hand around hers over his cock. Their groans mixed until he was bucking and she was stroking faster, harder.

"Fuck, yeah. I'm coming," he moaned.

She pulled harder and felt the sticky jet of his desire all over her hand while he whispered her name. She leaned back from him and looked down, enthralled with his large cock covered in cum.

"You made a mess," she teased and kissed his jaw.

"Shit." He was breathing hard and leaned his head back against the head rest. His eyes closed, and he sat there, panting.

"For such a bully, you're surprisingly sexy." She rubbed his seed over his semi-hard cock, wondering when she'd finally feel him inside her. "Now we're even."

He opened his eyes and looked at her. "Even?"

"For last night."

"Hell, no. We're not even." He tugged her hand from his cock and cleaned them both with a few tissues he grabbed from the tissue box on the floor. "I gave you an orgasm last night, and I made you dinner tonight. One measly orgasm from you is way less than I deserve."

She frowned while he buttoned up. "Measly? Nothing small about the mess you made in your lap. I'd say that was a whopper of an orgasm. Heck. You owe me another dinner for that handjob."

He just stared at her.

"What?"

"Hearing you say handjob. That innocent face and the sex

talk. I'm hard again."

"Shut up." She blushed. "Well, I suppose I should get going. My boss is an ogre, and if I'm late tomorrow, he'll probably fire me."

"Not if you blow him in the office. You know how many fantasies I've had of you on your knees, or bending you over my desk and—"

"*Goodnight*, Mac." She scooted away and yanked on the door handle.

He stopped her before she could leave. "For the record, we're not even. When I'm coming deep inside you and you're crying out my name? Then we'll be even."

"Well when will that be?" she asked, annoyed he seemed to be toying with her. "Why wait? Let's just get it over with." She wanted to end her sexual dormancy with the man, and he didn't seem to be getting the hint.

"Get it over with?" He scowled. "Seriously, Doran. You need help with that attitude. Make sure to wear something tight tomorrow."

Interesting how natural it felt to revert to their previous roles as combatants. She liked that she felt at ease with him. After their recent intimacy, she would have thought she'd be blushing and stammering. Yet Mac made it all seem normal to be so close to him. "Don't be an ass, Jameson."

"It's okay, honeybuns. I'm *your* ass for the time being." He smiled and wiggled his brows. "Now get inside. It's cold out. And don't be late tomorrow."

She left the car and slammed the door on his laughter. But he was right. It was cold outside. She hustled inside the Victorian and locked the door behind her. Then she peered through the dormer curtains, not surprised he'd waited until he'd seen her inside before he left.

Mac Jameson. An ass. A dictator. A skilled lover. A true puzzle she had every intention of figuring out. *Because he's a potential friend with benefits and nothing more.*

And wasn't that what she wanted? No more emotional pitfalls, just a sexy man with whom she could end her dry spell. So why did she sense her date with Mac as the beginning of so much more?

CHAPTER SIX

MAC THOUGHT HE'D DONE AN IMPRESSIVE JOB BY holding out last night. He hadn't jumped Maggie when he'd seen her wearing those form-hugging jeans and pretty pink tee. When she'd fallen asleep on him, he'd been the perfect gentleman, even though her breasts had been pressing into his side and giving him the hard-on from hell.

And even when she'd come on to him in the SUV, he hadn't done more than let her handle him, when every cell in his body had demanded *he* take charge, put her in the back of the vehicle, and fuck the shit out of her.

He blew out a breath. *So far, so good, Jameson.*

As the morning flew by and Maggie did no more than scowl at him before tending to her class, Mac felt on even keel once more. Though the day passed by with agonizing slowness, he didn't feel as if he'd damaged their relationship, such as it was. He got hives just thinking about the R word, but with Maggie, he defined it as a friendship first, one that would hopefully lead to some fucking incredible sex. He just needed

68

to layer the trust between them, to see if the subtle submissive vibes he'd sensed rang true.

For all that the woman lashed out at him like a Doberman, she obeyed at the oddest times, when she should have been protesting his control. Telling her what to do concerning their date? Taking charge of her climax the other night? She'd melted for him. And he just knew she'd be perfect on her knees, obeying him.

That's *if* he could get her there.

Stubborn thing would make him work to own her. Yet he looked forward to the challenge. Nothing worth having in life had ever been easy. And sure as shit, Maggie Doran screamed *difficult*.

He watched her leave work, heard more chatter about her fine ass, and did his best to steer clear of the women who tended to want more of his attention than he felt comfortable giving.

Normally he didn't mind their flattery. He admitted it soothed his bruised ego, considering Maggie hadn't come on to him before he'd made his move. Knowing she'd been celibate helped cool his ardor, but not by much. After their last two days spent with each other, he knew he could seal the deal and make a memory with her he'd never forget.

Yet he didn't think he'd given them enough time to really know each other. The woman thought he had trust issues? Learning she'd been abandoned as a kid offered some valuable insight. Shelby had been less than forthcoming, and Shane's knowledge of the blond beauty was limited to what Shelby had shared with him, which wasn't much more than what Mac had already known. Mac's future lover had an older brother named Trevor. She worked at an art gallery called The Beholder for a woman named Kim. She designed paper sculptures and worked part time teaching aerobics to make ends meet.

He also knew that she spent a lot of time with Shelby and Mimi Vanzant, Shelby's Mom, whom Mac had met and taken an instant liking to.

Mimi took flamboyancy to a whole new level, but she had a heart nearly as big as her personality. Just like her best friend. Although Ron's inspection had made him uncomfortable the first few times he'd encountered the guy, he'd adjusted. Mac didn't have a problem with gays. He'd had his share of men come on to him, and he'd easily rebuffed the offers, no harm no foul. He couldn't care less about orientation. Something his uncle had made sure to drill into his head early on. It wasn't about looks, status, or background, but about action. If a Marine worked hard, color, race, sexuality, and gender mattered little. Now, if the Marine fucked around on the job, Mac stepped in and kicked some serious ass.

Unlike Ron who apparently liked *fucking* ass. Sex with a dude did nothing for Mac, but with a woman?

Mac had tried anal a few times with past girlfriends. He wasn't opposed to it, but he preferred a nice tight pussy. Yet he'd had some tasty fantasies about taking Maggie anywhere and everywhere. The woman made him hard by just breathing. The thought of owning her fine ass, of coming in her pussy or better yet, her mouth, just seemed like something he *had* to do.

How many more dates before he saw the green light in her gaze? And not as something to *get over with*, but something to savor?

"There you are." Shane guffawed from the doorway to Mac's office. "Down boy. Happy to see me?" He glanced at Mac's crotch, which as usual, stood at attention at thoughts of Maggie.

Mac quickly sat behind his desk and flushed. "I was

daydreaming about Maggie. Happy?"

"Not as happy as you, apparently." Shane closed the door of Mac's office behind him and sat across from Mac's desk to face him. "So how did Saturday night go? You've been way too quiet about it."

"It went okay after I scared the shit out of her."

"Figured you might. Maggie doesn't have a lot of guys over, or so Shelby says. She wouldn't have been expecting anyone else to be there."

"Yeah, well, after she got over her near stroke, I left. We had dinner last night."

Shane's eyes widened, as did his grin. "Oh?"

"So what?" Mac tried for blasé, but Shane wasn't having it.

"You like her. *A lot.* This isn't just lust. I know you, buddy. You normally fuck 'em and leave 'em. Sorry to say."

"As I said before, so what? The ladies know what they're in for. Hell, that's why they come to me. They want a fun ride, and I give it to them."

"Yeah? So did you bone her yet?"

"Don't be an ass. And since when do you talk like me? 'Bone her?'"

Shane stood and pointed at Mac. "A ha!"

"What the fuck does that mean?"

"You want Maggie as something more than a fuck toy. Amen. The boy has finally grown up."

"I'm a desk away from putting your face through my wall," Mac warned, thoroughly aggravated. Yeah, he liked Maggie. But Shane made it sound a lot more serious than the emotion warranted. Mac just wanted to dominate her a little, and to do that, he wanted a tighter friendship between them. They'd have sex, then go their separate ways. No biggie.

Shane smiled widely. "Dude, you and my idiot brother

71

gave me so much dicked up advice about Shelby, it's a wonder the woman still talks to me. Thankfully, she's learned to ignore both of you. I think she might be considering moving in with me."

"You asked her?"

"Yeah. We talk about the next step a lot. I'm, ah, going to ask her to marry me at Christmas."

"Congrats." Mac gave him a thumbs up. "Not as big a pussy as you look. It's about time."

"Shut up." His buddy grinned. "But we were talking about you and Maggie."

"No, *we* weren't. *You* were."

Shane ignored his annoyance. "Yep. You were full of *great* advice when it came to Shelby. I was supposed to use her and lose her. I wasn't supposed to commit, or else I'd be stuck in another relationship."

"And here you are, Mr. Feelings. Like a woman, but with a dick."

"Nice mouth."

He wanted to say, *Maggie seems to like it.* But he didn't want to talk about her like that. *What the fuck is that all about?*

"See? There's that look. You're introspective now."

"Shut the hell up. I have work to do."

Shane crowed. "You're into her. Wait until I tell Shelby."

Mac rushed around the desk and put Shane in a headlock until he cried uncle. "Not a word to your girlfriend, you get me?"

"F-fine. Let...me...go."

Mac released him and rested his back against the door, blocking Shane's exit. "I'm working my way slowly with Maggie. Like you said, she's a nice woman." *Nice.* The blond was a shark in tights. "She's also Shelby's best friend. I happen to like your girlfriend, so I can't afford to have Maggie hate me." *Yeah, like that's the only reason I'm worried about screwing up with her. It has nothing to do with the fact that I actually like spending time with her. More than is healthy.* "Don't fuck it up for me, Shane."

Shane rubbed his throat, still grinning, the idiot. "No, sir. But I have to tell you. The fact you aren't trying to get straight into her pants is a sign."

Worried because he had a feeling Shane was right, Mac swore again.

"Talk to me, Goose."

"What is your need to talk about every damn thing?" Mac sneered. "I hate when you quote *Top Gun*. Fucking squid movie." The Navy had nothing on the Corps.

"Look, what's the problem here? So you like her. You date, fine. It works or it doesn't. That's life."

So why did Mac worry about the not working part? He didn't want to think about not being able to argue with her at the gym when she worked. And he couldn't believe how much he looked forward to seeing her. Even without the sex, he liked being with her. For Maggie he'd consider going to a freakin' coffee shop and sitting around, bullshitting with the other metrosexuals.

Jesus. He really needed to get laid.

"She's not bitchy or a money-grubber," Shane was saying. "You can trust her, and hell, I like her. She's hot, has a job— has *two* jobs—and her own place, and is friends with my girlfriend. I mean, what's not to like? So why all the worry?"

Maybe Shane could help him. He did tend to think like a woman. "Because I think with her I'll want more, but I don't know if it'll scare her off or not."

Shane blinked. "More as in… Oh, *more*." Shane knew about Mac's proclivities toward dominance. They'd talked about it a few times, and Shane had tried the D/s thing with his ex but hadn't found it satisfying. Personally, Mac loved it. But partners into his kind of kink were hard to come by, and he didn't want an anonymous hook up at a sex club. He'd been there, done that. Mac was tired of vanilla. He wanted sex that felt right, and he wanted to explore that path with Maggie.

"What if she isn't into it? Think that would throw you off?" Shane asked.

"I don't know." The crux of the matter. Mac had always known exactly what he wanted in a steady partner. His ultimate fantasy girl would have to be strong and independent away from him. He didn't want to babysit and had no urge to deal with a 24/7 slave. But in the bedroom, he wanted to dominate. He wanted a woman to crawl to him, to satisfy his needs because she wanted to. She would want him to care for her and pleasure her because she'd know that turned him on. An equal and fulfilling exchange.

He couldn't remember the last time he'd felt that with anyone. Maybe he never had, but he had the urge to fit Maggie into that role. *One step at a time, moron. You haven't even fucked her yet. Why not take it slow before you scare her off?* His hormones were totally screwing with him.

"You should see the misery on your face." Shane looked gleeful, until Mac glared at him again. Shane lost the smugness, but not the pleasure behind his words. "It's about time you found a decent woman. Give it a shot. Like you said, take it slow. My bet is you end up falling hard for her. Then all that Dom shit won't matter, because you'll be in love."

"Go easy on all the love talk, Nancy."

Shane laughed. "Whatever. You should try it sometime. A woman you actually like outside the bedroom can be a ton of fun. Look, I feel sorry for you. If you want, you can double with me and Shelby to take off the pressure. You said you wanted a different kind of relationship than the ones you normally have. No fucking and flying," he said, repeating Mac's earlier comments.

"I know. I'm being careful with her. We haven't had sex yet." Not exactly.

"Which for you is a miracle."

"Don't you have somewhere else to be?" Mac growled. "It's six thirty."

"Oh, right." Shane flipped him a one-finger salute. "Heading back to my place, where my hot, sexy girlfriend will be waiting for me with dinner."

The lucky bastard. Mac shrugged. "Yeah? Well I'm going home to a crotchety old man with control issues."

"Sounds like you and your future are closer than you think." Shane laughed. "Tell your uncle I said hi."

"Yeah, yeah. Give Shelby a kiss for me."

"Dream on."

"Later, slacker." Mac watched his buddy leave and decided he'd worked long enough. After letting his night manager know he was taking off, he drove home for a family dinner, which usually consisted of Mac slaving away while his uncle nagged him about something. Hopefully Ian would remember to bring some beer this time.

He saw his uncle's truck parked in front of the house and pulled into the driveway. The door opened and his uncle held up a six pack of Mac's favorite microbrew.

"Come on, boy. I brought pizza. Well, get the lead out." Ian slammed the door shut.

Mac smiled. Maybe tonight wouldn't be a total waste. Pizza and beer would go a long way toward making Ian's lecture easier to bear.

♥

Just shoot me now.

Maggie swallowed another sigh as Mimi waved her hands above her head, the bangles clanging like it was the fourth of July. Shelby grinned at her with evil intent.

"I thought you and Shane had planned on a quiet night at home," Maggie accused.

"Nah. I left him a note. He has the house to himself tonight. I wanted to spend more time with you, best buddy." Shelby turned a bright smile on her mother. "And then I thought about how long it's been since I had dinner with Mom and Ron too, and here we are."

In hell.

Maggie knew what this was about. Payback. Just because Maggie had, with the best of intentions, interfered in Shelby's love life, Shelby now felt like she had to do the same to Maggie. But Shelby didn't seem to understand Maggie didn't want her help—or maybe Shelby did. The woman could hold a grudge.

"Now, dear. Tell me more about Mac Jameson," Mimi said to Maggie.

Ron dug into his noodles. "He's to-die-for handsome. All that muscle. Yum."

"I know that. I've met the man, like a Greek god to us mere mortals. I want to know what Maggie thinks of him." She turned to Maggie. "Well, dear? Is he a bit thick?"

Maggie choked on an egg roll. He'd felt like more than a handful to her.

"As in," Mimi continued, a merry glint in her eye, "can he handle a conversation, or is he as dense as a brick? Is he homophobic? Does he like color more than he used to? I swear, he wanted nothing more than wood tones for his home. Meh. I've only caught the bare minimum from our brief meetings. He's not the most patient of men."

"He likes Maggie's art," Shelby added. "I'm pretty sure he's not homophobic. I don't know his favorite color, but from what I do know, he's a great guy. He's been nice to me."

"Because you're dating his best friend," Maggie pointed out. "He's okay if you're into the muscle-bound, control-freak type."

"Sounds right up your alley," Shelby answered.

"But I'm not in the market for a man. I'm concentrating on finishing a few more projects for the gallery. Kim has a buyer coming in January. He's already expressed interest in a few pieces she put on the website. She thinks he might want to put some in his galleries on the East Coast."

"That would be wonderful." Mimi beamed. "You should focus wholeheartedly on your work. Shelby, quit bugging the girl."

Shelby stared. "You're kidding, right? You three stuck your big noses in my business not that long ago."

"Out of love," Ron reminded her. "Maggie seems to have a head on her shoulders. You, sadly, were hopeless."

"He's right." Maggie grinned. "You were so pathetic about your ex that you couldn't see what a great guy Shane is. You should be thanking us."

"True." Mimi stared at Shelby, waiting. Then she sighed. "Stubborn girl. Fine. Don't thank me." Ron cleared his throat, and she amended, "Don't thank *us*. But Maggie, you I trust. You could have any man you wanted if you had the time to pursue one. Don't you worry about a thing."

Maggie breathed easier. They finished dinner and she left to use the restroom. Thank God Mimi had a little faith in her.

"I can't believe you," Shelby whispered in a mean voice. "Maggie is totally pathetic. She's planning to be the next neighborhood cat lady, for God's sake."

"Relax." Ron slicked back his hair. He looked so handsome and so happy, mostly because of the perpetual smile he wore since he'd begun dating Shane's boss, Justin. Personally, Shelby thought things might grow serious between them. She wondered how her mother would handle her best friend finding a happily ever after without her.

Ron continued. "What your mother meant is that we'll find Maggie a man since she's so busy with her career. Isn't that right, Mimi?"

"Reads me like an open book." Mimi laughed and gave him an air kiss. "Now this Jameson. He's rarely stuck around when I've been near. Why is that?"

Shelby wanted to crow with satisfaction. "Probably because he works a lot." *And no doubt Shane warned him to steer clear of you if he wanted to retain his sanity.* "He's a terrific guy. A little too buff for me, but he's exactly Maggie's type. Problem is she won't open up and give him a chance. And he really seems to like her." Shelby saw Maggie exit the hall to the restrooms and lowered her voice. "Shane seems to think his friend is head over heels for her, just too stubborn to admit it."

Mimi glanced over her shoulder, saw Maggie, and whispered back to Shelby, "Then you sit back and let Ron and me handle this. That's if Justin isn't taking all your free time?" she asked with a sneer.

"Green with envy, yet still beautiful."

"Don't get that tone with me," Mimi warned him.

"Maggie's coming," Shelby reminded them.

"Fine. I'll handle Jameson." Mimi huffed. "You two keep

your men happy and I'll stay out of your lives. But Ron, if Justin breaks your heart, I'll break him in half."

"Oh, so sweet. No wonder I love you."

Mimi sighed. "All the good ones are either taken or gay, I keep telling you. Be thankful you have a good man, Shelby. Now let's help our spiritual daughter find some testosterone to love."

They were toasting and laughing as Maggie reached the table.

"Guess I missed all the fun."

When they laughed harder, she frowned. But that suspicion wouldn't help her. Shelby shook her head. Once her mother scented a man, she never stopped until she bagged her prey. Poor, poor Maggie.

Payback was a bitch.

CHAPTER SEVEN

MAGGIE SPENT THE NEXT WEEK TRYING NOT TO OBSESS about Mac. When he wasn't ripping her a new one for some imagined infraction at the gym, she didn't see him. Both relieved and upset about it, she threw herself into work. She hadn't lied to Mimi and the others about needing to deliver.

She had three projects near completion, and two she'd recently turned over to Kim. With only two weeks left until Christmas and so much more to do, Maggie shouldn't have had time to worry about a man she didn't classify as date-worthy, even if she had been in a dating frame of mind. Mac would be great at sex, but she couldn't see him catering to a woman's emotional needs. Though he'd surprised her by being deeper than she'd first assumed, she still couldn't envision going to a movie or a bookstore with him as anything but painful.

From what she'd seen, he was a man's man. A tits and ass, muscles and fitness ex-Marine who liked cars and guy things—which still baffled Maggie. The Speed Channel and vehicular fun had never done a thing for her.

And why the hell am I thinking about him again? She huffed a frustrated breath and finished with her latest sculpture, a shifting piece in blues and greens that made her think of the ocean. Maggie did her own framing, and she finished tacking a nail into the back of her frame and set it with the others.

One down, two to go. A glance at the clock convinced her to take a break until tomorrow. After she trudged back inside her apartment and had a quick shower, she threw on her robe and dried her hair, unable to sleep on a wet head during the winter. She hadn't done much more than blow it dry. A glance in the mirror showed a sleepy looking blue-eyed blond in a soft but tattered purple robe that all but swallowed her in it. Pleased she would make her deadline next week, she decided to treat herself to some wine. Looking forward to her first free Saturday in a month, she decided to celebrate.

She poured herself a glass and started a fire. Her favorite television show aired in another ten minutes, and for once she wasn't asleep or behind on work, so she'd enjoy it.

Settling under a warm blanket with the wine by her side on the table and the low murmur of the television, she'd found Nirvana.

And then someone knocked on her door.

"Damn." Probably Shelby wanting to hang out. Shane must have ditched her. The guy spent every waking moment with Shelby as it was, so Maggie didn't begrudge him his private time. But that left Shelby at loose ends, and Maggie had really been looking forward to having her own space tonight.

The knock came again.

"Hold on," she called out and tossed off her blanket. She trudged to the floor in wool socks and peered through the peep hole. She froze. After a moment, she opened the door. "Yes?"

Mac Jameson stood in the communal hallway of the aging Victorian looking edible in jeans and a black leather jacket. In the hall lighting, his bright blue eyes glinted with some

Marie Harte

indefinable emotion.

"Here. These are for you." He held out a bouquet of pink roses.

"Ah, what?"

The intensity on his face faded, and a smile took the place of his frown. "That is one ugly robe."

"Hey!"

He stepped forward and would have trampled her if she hadn't moved back. Before she knew it, he'd entered her apartment and closed and locked the door behind him.

"Nice trick."

"It's called being persuasive." He put the flowers in her hand and closed her fingers over the smooth stems.

"You brought me flowers?" Mystified, she didn't know what to think. Was this another part of his nonsexual dating technique?

"You want them or not?"

"Yes, yes." She hugged them to her when he moved to take them back. Flowers. When was the last time a man had brought her roses? "Such an ungrateful gift giver. Thank you. I love them."

She turned and left to rummage in the kitchen for a vase. After she'd arranged and watered them, she put them in the center of her dining table. "So pretty." She glanced up to see Mac right in front of her. "Mac?"

"Yeah. So pretty," he rumbled and tugged her to him using her belt.

Her robe parted just as he planted a warm, hungry kiss on her mouth. Maggie could only kiss him back, caught up in an inferno of unfulfilled desire. Everything inside her hungered for the magic of a man who didn't hesitate to take what he wanted.

He broke the kiss and ran his mouth down her neck.

82

"What are you wearing under this?"

"N-nothing."

He tensed and pulled back. "Are you fucking kidding me?"

"I just took a shower." She frowned, wondering what it took to break the man's resolve.

"I am so screwed," she thought she heard him mutter under his breath. In a louder voice, he said, "I came over to say hi. You've been avoiding me this week, and I wanted to make sure we were still good."

"I was only keeping my distance from a crabby boss with control issues."

"Yeah, about those issues… Thing is, I want to fuck you."

"O-kay." The man's thoughts shifted like the wind. "And this makes you crabby because…?"

"Because what I want from you is a little different from what you're probably used to. I want us to get to know each other better so you'll feel okay about sleeping with me, *my* way."

She caught her breath. "Spell it out. What exactly do you want me to do with you?"

"Everything I want, exactly the way I want it." He tilted her chin up so that he could look straight into her eyes. "I want to play games with you. Ones where we need a safeword. Where you call me Sir and you obey me." He kissed her again, and she felt her robe begin to open. Then his hands were inside, stroking her heated flesh. "I want to own your body in bed. Would you be willing to let me do that?"

"All this for some roses?" she replied while trying to make sense of her dreams suddenly meshing with reality.

He chuckled. "Nah. The roses were to show you I was thinking of you." He cupped her breasts, and his eyes darkened. "But this is way more than I'd planned on asking for." He fully parted her robe and stared down at her. Slowly, he bent his head and took a flushed, pert nipple in his mouth.

He sucked hard, and her knees buckled. She moaned and hung on to him for dear life.

Mac turned his attention to her other breast and teased and nipped until she teetered on an orgasm. She'd never been so sensitive before, but moisture coated the insides of her thighs.

"Yeah. This is what I want. You helpless in my arms." He kissed her, his tongue penetrating while his hands moved down to cage her waist. "Maggie... *fuck*. I wanted to wait, but no more. I want you, but I'll go easy with my demands." He gripped her tight and kissed her again. "What do you think?"

She stared up at him when he pulled away. Her robe hung open, but he looked only at her eyes.

"I think... I think we should go back to my bedroom." She tugged him with her, sure only that the time had come to finally have Mac Jameson. Tomorrow could take care of itself. Tonight belonged to her.

Maggie drew him into her bedroom and stood, uncaring about her near nudity.

Mac's gaze wandered from her head to her toes and lingered in between. "You are fucking gorgeous."

She flushed, pleased and embarrassed with the praise. She'd always had a nice figure and attractive face, but her workouts had toned her body into an especially tight form.

"So you're good with doing things my way?" he ventured when he met her gaze again. "I'm not kidding around. I don't want to hurt you or anything, but I'd like to see if we fit the way I'd imagined."

He'd thought about her. Fantasized about her. She wondered if they had the same kinds of needs. "This isn't a joke, is it?"

His gaze softened. "No, honey. I want you, but I'm not an easy lover. I could pretend I like it simple, the way I normally do. But it's not enough, and lately, I need something more. I like to be in control, to take and demand. But I need to know if you can handle that. If you can't, it's okay." But she could sense the disappointment waiting behind her potential refusal. "I still want you. I just thought this might be something we'd both enjoy."

"Why would you think that?"

"You like me bossing you around. I've seen the way you react."

"H-how?"

"Your nipples get hard. You flush, those cheeks turning a pretty pink. And your pupils get bigger—all signs of arousal. You want to be mussed and controlled, don't you, Maggie?"

She did. And now he knew. She let out a breath. "What do you want me to do?"

He didn't smile or nod. He lost the easiness of expression and growled, "Take off your robe."

She shrugged out of it, and it pooled to the floor. Mac remained in his coat, completely dressed. The disparity wasn't lost on her. He wanted control, and God, she wanted to give it to him. Vulnerable and naked, she looked even smaller next to his powerful body.

"Now come and take off my jacket." He waited.

She swallowed and approached, feeling timid yet powerful at the same time. So strange.

She unzipped his coat, and the sound was overly loud in the quiet room. He watched her while she undressed him. She put the jacket on the chair next to her bed and waited.

Mac kissed her, so suddenly and with so much feeling she

could barely hold on. She gripped his arms and held tight while he plundered her mouth. Against her, his clothing scratched. His body had no give, his mouth no regret.

He pulled back and looked at her with a mean smile. "This is going to take a while. You don't have anywhere to go tomorrow, do you?"

"No," she said between pants. "My day off."

"Good." He kissed his way to her breasts before looking back at her, and she saw a new side to Mac she hadn't seen before. A sexually controlling master.

She shivered.

"Cold?" he asked.

"N-no."

"Wet?" He didn't let her answer but pushed a finger between her folds and into her. "I guess I'm not the only one wanting this."

Dear Lord. "I never said you were."

"*Sir.* I never said you were, Sir."

She bit her lip and moaned, "Sir."

"That's nice." He sighed and kissed her until she wanted to melt all over him. "Take off my shirt. I want your hands on my skin and your mouth on my nipples."

She liked him telling her what to do. Even better, she liked following his orders. He ground his pelvis against her and drew her attention to the raging erection beneath the denim.

Mac wanted her, no question.

Maggie drew his shirt off and placed it next to his jacket. She couldn't look away from his chest, those huge biceps and corded forearms. The man was seriously built, enough that it would be easy for him to hold her down and do whatever he wanted to her.

"What's that look?" he asked.

"You're so strong," she whispered. "So much bigger than me."

"Sir," he added, teasing.

"Sir." She kissed his chest, past the smattering of hair to the coppery disks of his nipples. She traced his muscles with her hands, loving the feel of his straining pectorals and ripped abdomen honed by hundreds of sit-ups and countless workouts at the gym. She drew on his nipples and kissed and licked, wanting to make him as crazy as she felt, until he yanked her back by her hair. The small bite of pain intrigued her, because she'd never thought she'd be into hurting at all.

The experience felt unreal, the way she'd imagined it so many times. It was like she'd conjured him out of her darkest fantasies.

He was no longer Mac, she no longer Maggie. Instead, Sir and his submissive played their fun and games. She moaned, losing herself in the woman she'd always wanted to be.

"I said let go," he growled.

She hadn't heard him. "Sorry. I didn't hear you."

"Being bad already? I think we need that safeword."

Maggie nodded, unable to look away from him. Punishment? She'd dreamed about that since she'd first read it in a novel. Spankings, pinches, maybe even a little biting. She'd never tried the kinkier stuff with any of her lovers, but she'd imagined doing it. So many times.

"Pick a word, Maggie." Mac pulled her closer by her hair, tilting her chin back to expose her neck. He sucked at her pulse and nibbled his way to her cheek. The small bites stung and made her wetter.

"Strawberry," she whispered. "That's my safeword."

"Good. You say that if you feel like we need to stop. I'll respect that boundary." He stared into her eyes. "I'm not bullshitting about that. You say *no*, I'll keep going. *Stop, wait*, those don't mean anything. The minute you say *strawberry*, I'll cease, no question. Say it for me."

"Strawberry."

"And don't be afraid to say it. I don't think you'll need it tonight, but I want to be safe." He paused. "And speaking of safe… You said you're on birth control?"

She nodded, glad to have this conversation. A lot of guys felt weird about condoms, but she'd rather be protected from the onset.

"I know you haven't had sex in a while."

She frowned at his grin.

"Now, now. Don't be embarrassed." His grin faded. "I haven't gotten laid in four long-ass months." He glared at her. "Some tight ass at the gym has been messing with my head."

She blinked at him. "Really?"

"Really, Sir." He pinched her nipple.

"*Sir*," she breathed.

"That hurt. And you liked it, didn't you?" he asked.

"Yes, Sir."

Mac closed his eyes for a moment then opened them. "Jesus, Maggie. You're incredible." He took a deep breath then let it out. "I've always worn a condom. Well, with the women I've been with in the past. I won't lie. I've dated a good bit. But nothing lasted." His eyes darkened. "I want to come inside you. You okay with that? I'm clean, but you can't know for sure. So if you want me to wear a rubber, I will."

"I trust you." She didn't have to think about it. With her safety, her job, even sex, she trusted him. That he wouldn't hurt her emotionally was a completely different story. But she wouldn't have to worry about that if they just had sex. Not making love, just sliding tab B into slot A. Period.

"Thank God." He grinned. "Now, little sub, get back to what you were doing. Touch me. And then we'll get started on my pants."

Mac swore as she embraced her role. Maggie Doran had been starring in his nightly fantasies for a while. But the reality far surpassed his imagination. She hungrily sucked his nipples, and he'd been sporting a hard-on that could split wood since he'd seen her in that ugly robe. Fuck, but he'd been hard-pressed not to ram himself in her and just come.

He needed the respite, but this torturous road to pleasure felt so much better. He liked depriving himself. Plus it let him see how much of her he could take.

The woman played hell on his control. He'd never been so close to losing it from some heavy petting and kissing. For that reason he'd remained dressed long after he would have gotten naked with anyone else.

He ordered her to stop, and she pulled away looking dazed. Those tits swayed, and she panted, in lust. *For him.* "Now my pants. I want you to take your time. You're not to touch my cock. Just get my clothes off."

Or he'd lose it. Coming in two seconds wouldn't impress her. And he needed to show her he was worthy of ordering her around. He remained still, lifting his legs only to help her after she removed his shoes and socks. When her hands moved to his fly, it was all he could do to remain still. She finally had his jeans around his knees. But when she shifted to completely remove them, her cheek brushed against his underwear, sliding down his erection.

A damp spot clearly indicated how much he wanted her. His slit had been wet since he'd seen her large nipples. And that taut belly... Her pussy was drool-worthy. She had a thin strip of hair on her mound, making for easy access when he ate her out. In the next two seconds if she didn't hurry.

"Quit playing, Maggie."

She took off his jeans and underwear and turned to put them on the chair. He wouldn't let her turn back around.

"Don't move. That's it. Bend over the chair and spread your legs."

"Yes, Sir." Man, her breathy voice really did it for him.

"More. Thrust your hips back. That's it." Christ, he could see her wet thighs and pussy. All that cream just for him.

He couldn't wait any longer. Mac covered her like a stallion and slid his cock between her folds. Not inside her, but against her, and the friction only whetted his appetite for more.

She bucked under him, and he held her still with his much larger frame. "Ever been ass fucked, little sub?" He wanted to take that small hole in the worst way. Because it, and every other part of her, was his. Anal with other women had never been a big deal. With Maggie, it made claiming her that much more complete.

"No, Sir."

"Then we'll have to remedy that. But not tonight." He humped her, sliding between her cleft but not penetrating. Not yet. "You're so hot and wet. You feel good."

He hugged her, cupping her breasts and making sure to graze her clit with each pass of his cock.

"Please, Mac. God, more."

"What's that?"

"I mean *Sir*."

"Naughty." And time for him to back off before he came. He let her go. "Get on the bed on your back. Spread your legs wide."

She hurried to obey. Nothing timid about her now. She

wanted to be fucked. Needed to be ridden hard. But he wasn't about to stop playing yet.

Mac let her have a good look at him. "See this?" He held himself and stroked a few times, aware she bit her lower lip with desire. So sexy. He wanted her to suck his dick but knew if she did their time would be over before it began. "This is all for you, Maggie. For my little sub."

"I want you inside me, Sir."

"*You* want?" He shook his head. "It's what *I* want that matters."

She quickly nodded. "Yes, Sir. Whatever you want."

"I want to taste you."

Her eyes widened.

"That's right." He released his hold on his cock and joined her on the bed, kneeling between her legs. "I want to eat *my* pussy. Show me where it aches, sub."

Maggie moaned, arched her head back, and put her hand over her pussy. "Here, Sir."

"No, don't point to it. Touch yourself. Let me see that clit. Hold yourself open for me."

She spread her lower lips, showing her glistening, engorged clitoris. "Please, Sir."

"Good girl." Mac levered closer and closed his mouth over her. She tasted wild, a spice that went straight to his head and made him dizzy with the need to take. She cried out and fisted the bed, and he sucked harder, wanting to make her crazed. "Don't come yet, sub. Wait for Master to let you."

She moaned, and he knew she was as into the fantasy as he was. Giving and taking, sharing the dream of possession that swung both ways.

He'd been right not to rush this. From the first moment he'd seen her, he'd wanted her. But she hadn't known him at all. He couldn't imagine she'd have let him fuck her like this. Yet now he had her under him, writhing for his mouth.

He sucked harder, flicking her clit with his tongue and nibbling with his teeth. He gripped her inner thighs hard, grazing the tender flesh as he slid his fingers toward her ass. Her thighs were slick from the moisture coating her pussy, and he eased his thumb through her natural lube and settled the tip of his thumb at her asshole.

While he nipped her clit with his teeth, he pushed into her ass.

"Please. More," she begged, breathless.

Yet in her passion, she failed to call him by name. He pulled back and slapped her pussy hard enough to shock but not hard enough to actually hurt. Then he shoved two fingers inside her.

Maggie cried out and came, coating him with a rush of slick release. Her moans and mewls of pleasure sent a rush of hunger through his blood.

"That's fucking hot. Even if you are a bad sub," Mac growled. "You weren't told you could come yet, were you?" Excited at the thought of punishing her, he removed his fingers, aware she tried to clamp down on them.

"I'm sorry…Sir," She said as she tried to catch her breath.

"Not sorry enough." The woman looked like a goddamn angel, flushed with repletion, her eyes cloudy, her lips rosy red and swollen from his kisses. "You ever deep-throated, sub?"

She swallowed hard, and the action had his cock jerking. "Y-yes, Sir."

"You were a bad girl. And bad girls get punished."

"I'm sorry, Sir. I deserve to be punished."

"You don't look sorry." She looked fucking sexy as hell. Mac straddled her body and walked on his knees up her frame, so that he stopped with his balls just over her mouth. "Suck me."

She didn't argue at all, but latched onto him and laved him with her tongue while sucking as ordered. She gripped his thighs with her hands, holding on while she worshipped him with her mouth. Fuck if he could think of anything but taking her everywhere. He wanted to come in her mouth, pussy and ass at the same time. Completely impossible, but the thought nearly did him in.

He rocked over her, trying desperately to hang on. "No," he said hoarsely and pulled back. "Open up. Take me to the back of your throat, and feel free to gag," he ordered, wondering if this would push her too far. He hesitated, wanting to give her time to use that safe word if she needed to, while every part of his oversensitive body protested the delay.

"Yes, Master," she whispered and opened her mouth wide.

Master. "Shit." Mac angled over her and inched his way inside her mouth. "Breathe through your nose," he rasped and continued to thrust. "Swallow me. Draw me in. I'm coming down your throat, pretty sub. So fucking hard."

He wanted to last, but he could still taste her on his lips. And as he stared down at her, those red lips hugging his cock, he lost it. Mac pumped twice before ramming hard and coming. He groaned as he jetted into her mouth, loving the tiny gagging sound she made while swallowing him.

To know she wasn't comfortable yet obeyed anyway gave him a heady sense of relief. They could do this. Play and fuck and enjoy one another. He withdrew on a shudder and wiped a few drops of leftover cum onto her lips.

"Lick it off," he said in a deep voice and watched with pleasure as she arched her head off the pillow to take one more drop off his cock. She wiped her lips clean with that soft pink tongue, the one he wanted to feel licking his slit again. Mac controlled a shudder. "You okay?"

"You're big, Sir." She blew out a breath. "But taking you like that was really sexy. I liked it." She paused and blushed. "Sir."

That shyness in contrast with the stacked blond supplicant beneath him... Her demure expression screamed submissive, and he wanted like hell to own her for more than tonight, but a lot longer than that.

More than was healthy, no doubt.

Mac stared down at her, wondering what to do next. He hadn't brought any of his favorite toys to use on her, because he hadn't figured they'd have sex tonight. But hell. On the off chance she changed her mind tomorrow, he wanted to experience all that he could. He *had* to.

"That was just foreplay, baby. Now how about you turn over and show Master that fine ass."

CHAPTER EIGHT

MAGGIE BRACED HERSELF ON HER HANDS AND KNEES, stunned Mac could have the energy to go again after that mind-numbing orgasm. Well, after hers, anyway. She couldn't be sure what he felt, but he'd come for an awful long time down her throat.

Oh my God. I deep-throated my boss! She wanted to hysterically giggle, but then he slapped her ass, and the burn shocked her.

"That's a pretty pink," he said in that gravelly voice that did funny things to her insides.

He was so big, so commanding. She sensed him looming behind her, could feel the hair on his legs brushing against the backs of her thighs. And then his cock, that semi-hard wonder brushing her asshole.

"I'm going to fuck this pretty hole, baby."

"No." An automatic denial, yet she shivered with excitement at the same time.

He continued as if she hadn't spoken. With another two slaps to her ass, he had her crying out in pain. "Nice. I like that.

Did it hurt, sub?"

He was so good at this. Not playing a part, but living it with her in the moment. She had no focus for anything but Mac, her master, behind her. For so long she'd dreamed about an experience like this. She didn't want it to end.

"Yes, Sir. A feel-good hurt, though, Sir."

"Good." He rubbed his cock between her legs, coating himself in her release. "You gave me a nice orgasm, sub. Enough to work off my need. So now when I fuck your ass, it won't be so rough. Isn't that nice of Master?"

"Y-yes, Sir." She swayed under him, breathless, excited, and scared of having that huge cock up her ass. Maggie hadn't had anal sex in years, and the one time she'd tried it had been less than stellar. That guy had been nowhere near Mac in size.

In one swift thrust, he entered her pussy once more and took her breath away.

"Shit. You're still hot. So wet." He moaned and stilled, and she swore she felt him grow.

When he stopped, she wriggled her hips to get him to move, and he clenched her waist tight.

"Stop. Let me…" He withdrew and thrust slowly. "That's it. My hard-on is back." He removed himself from her body and wiped her cream down to her ass. "You're wet enough. You'll have to be," he said softly.

She didn't like the sound of that. "But—"

He put himself at her anus and pushed. The small breach felt good, surprisingly erotic. And then he hit a ring of flesh that refused to give. It hurt.

"You didn't think that blowjob was your punishment, did you?" He laughed, a thick sound of angry need that turned her on without trying. "No, sub. You need a good ass-fucking."

She heard his excitement, and it amped her own. No

matter that she'd just come, she wanted to come again. With Mac in such a forbidden place, taking her from behind. She felt small and helpless under him. A totally foreign sense of self from the strong, independent Maggie. For some odd reason tears came to her eyes. Tears of relief, of confusion, but most of all, tears of joy.

"Accept Master. That's it." Mac thrust slowly, but he continued to move. "Push out and you'll take me easier." He sounded strangled. His fingers would leave bruises when he let her waist go, but the telling restraint eased a sigh out of her.

"Yes, Sir. Please, more." Her breath hitched when he continued to penetrate.

The burn grew, as did the fullness. Such a wicked thing, having him there. Yet she couldn't imagine anyone else owning her so completely. Dazed and taken, feeling completely under his spell, she trembled and waited for him to stop.

"You okay?" he rasped and finally ceased moving. "Christ, I'm in. All inside that tight, fuckable ass. You know how many times I used to dream about this? Every time you'd bend over in those tight shorts, every time you flaunted yourself after telling me to kiss your ass… I wanted to kiss it. To fuck it." He leaned over her back and seated himself deeper.

She moaned, hurting yet aroused all over again.

"Yeah. That's it." He kissed her shoulder and the small of her back. Then he let go of her waist to hold her shoulders. "Oh, that's good." Mac withdrew a little, which eased the pressure inside her. And then he thrust forward again, getting better penetration because he used her shoulders to grip her. "Yeah." He moaned and started fucking her, slowly, then faster as she moaned and pleaded for more.

More pain, more fucking, more feeling like a woman born to be owned.

"That's a good girl." He pumped harder, his balls slapping her pussy. "You feel good, Maggie."

Hearing her name cemented something between them. He wasn't imaging some other woman. No other *sub* or *baby*. She warmed and felt herself drift, lost in Mac and his hold over her body.

"Fuck. I'm gonna come. Right up inside you." He yanked her back against him, grinding against her hips as he groaned and came.

He didn't let her go, even after she felt him soften inside her.

Mac eased his hands from her shoulders, stroking her back and hips as he straightened on his knees behind her. "Shit. I left bruise marks on your hips."

"I like it, Sir." She felt drugged.

"Good. Because I like seeing them there." His satisfaction was hard to miss. "I left a lot of cum in you, sub. And you're going to let it stay there." He withdrew. "Get down on your belly while I go clean up."

He left her and returned with a damp rag. As Mac cleaned her with a gentle touch, she started to come down off her high.

"You good, baby?"

"Yes, Sir." She sighed. "I don't think I can move."

He chuckled and finished with the cloth. She closed her eyes, content to lie there, even when she started to feel the cold.

"Can't have you shivering." Mac pulled the covers out from under her and tucked them both in. After a few moments, when she'd just started to fall asleep, drugged on his warmth, he spoke again. "Maggie, you okay?"

"Mm-hmm."

"You'd tell me if you weren't, right? I mean, I'm your

master. I told you to tell me the truth. You're sure you're fine?"

"I said so, didn't I?" she wanted to snap but could barely think past the need to snuggle into his warmth.

"No discipline," she thought she heard him say before he sighed and spooned her against him.

Maggie woke the next morning disoriented. She'd had the best dream ever. Total submission to Mac Jameson, and he'd been the best master she could have hoped for. Domineering, overwhelming, and so strong.

Something hard and hot nudged her from behind.

No dream. That was totally real. Her mind blanked as she processed how she felt about him. Then she smiled. "I rock."

He chuckled against her neck and dragged her leg over his. On her side, she had little leverage to stop him. Not that she wanted to. When he thrust inside her and started fucking her, she didn't argue.

"That's it. Give it to me," he ordered as he demanded her pleasure. Mac filled her, stretching out her tight pussy and then rubbing her clit with a callused thumb. "Come for me, sub. Come hard."

She followed his lead, letting her body fall over the edge with him, caught in his pleasure as much as her own.

After a few moments, he withdrew and hauled her out of bed with him. "Time to shower." He made a face. "You're full of cum."

She snorted. "Your cum. And don't give me any more Master crap. We're out of bed. It's a new day." She had to put herself back on equal footing and fast, because Maggie felt wobbly. She wanted to continue the subservience thing, to see how far they could take it. But that meant getting deeper with Mac. Mind-blowing sex added to fulfilled fantasies of a guy she thought she might really like scared the crap out of her.

Marie Harte

"I knew you'd be like this." He sighed and dragged her into the bathroom. He turned toward the toilet and she hightailed it out of there.

"I am not watching you pee." That was way too intimate— a crazy thought considering what they'd done last night and this morning. But bathroom privileges meant relationship. *Not going there.*

After the toilet flushed and he came out with a frown, she pushed past him and locked herself in the bathroom.

"Hey," he shouted through the door.

"Hold on." After taking care of her needs, she turned on the shower, then let him back in. "Okay. Now we can shower."

"You're so controlling."

She had to laugh as they washed up. Maggie watched him soap those impressive muscles, turned on yet comfortable with him. Which was just weird.

Mac watched her just as intently. "Wash your tits. Yeah, play with your nipples until they get nice and hard." The spray of water covered his face, and drops clung to his lashes, making them look impossibly long. "I'm taking a mental picture." He grinned. "The next time you're giving me shit at work, just know I'll be seeing you naked and covered in water and bubbles."

She rinsed off. "Yeah? Well I'll be ignoring your demands at work. All the while I'll be remembering how good you were, coming in my ass. So big and full," she whispered. When he leaned close to kiss her, she shoved him back. "Uh uh. Playtime's over, big guy. I hate to kick you out, but I have work to do."

He blinked. "What?"

"Sorry. I had a lot of fun. I mean, you were great." She wanted to laugh at his crestfallen expression. Had he thought

100

she'd bow at his feet all weekend? She'd had an itch he'd more than scratched, as well as a dangerous warmth in her heart for the stubborn man. Not something she wanted to explore at the moment. She needed to get back to work. *And protect my heart,* whispered her sense of self-preservation.

Mac's frown slowly turned into a considering nod. "You've got a point. Time for me to go. I guess I'll see you at work tomorrow, huh?"

"Ah, right. Sunday." She had a class at four. A new step aerobics routine to work through with her experienced Sunday group before the rush returned on Monday.

Mac got out first, and Maggie took some extra time to compose herself before turning off the shower and stepping out. She dried off and dressed in her room, ignoring Mac while he watched her with eagle eyes.

"What?" she snapped.

He buttoned his jeans and threw on his shirt, then stopped to stare at her. "Embarrassed? Don't be, sweetness. You were terrific."

She knew that tone. Oddly enough, his arrogance soothed her. People who annoyed each other as much as she and Mac did would never have a relationship. Nothing meaningful, anyway. The sex, that she could handle.

"Thanks, hunk-of-love," she drawled. "You and that monster cock were impressive." Then to goad him, she added, "A little quick on the draw, but you said you'd been in a dry spell, like me. So that makes sense."

"Excuse me?"

Pleased she'd struck her target, she nodded. "Yeah. You really know how to work that Dom angle. Very sexy. You're big and thick. You definitely know how to use what you've got. I was just surprised you were so, um, quick. But it was good," she hastened to add.

"Yeah?" He glared at her, a familiar sight that turned her on all over again. "I'm thinking that next time you need a little more discipline. Some added punishment for being such a brat."

A next time. She wanted to clap with glee. Who said blonds were dumb? Maggie had finagled another sexual encounter with Mac without asking for one or looking vulnerable. Instead, she'd let his pride work in her favor. He'd make her pay, she was sure, but man, she couldn't wait.

She swallowed her satisfaction and finished dressing in her scrub clothes, what she normally wore when working in her makeshift studio. "Punish away if it makes you feel better, Mac."

He snarled something before leaving her bedroom and slamming out the front door.

Game set and match. Maggie laughed out loud before making herself some coffee. She hummed a Christmas carol under her breath and thought about getting a tree. Her good mood lasted throughout the weekend and into the next week.

♥

Two days later, Mac still had no idea where he'd gone wrong. He'd controlled the woman, had put her through her paces, and had the best damn orgasms of his life. She'd come hard too, had drenched him with her release and fallen asleep in his arms. A total girlfriend move that had freaked him out when he'd woken... until he'd felt her ass against his cock and had incredible morning sex.

So for her to dismiss him so casually, to have the nerve to accuse him of being "quick on the draw," made no sense that he could understand. No one criticized his technique. Not since the sexy widow O'Leary had shown him how to pleasure a woman, her graduation gift to the newly enlisted Marine, had Mac ever been close to being sexually lacking. And even then, Mrs. O'Leary had praised him for his enthusiasm.

"That little *witch*." The hell of it was, he still wanted to paddle Maggie's ass, then fuck her until she cried out his name. Somehow, she'd turned his dread of the morning after into a promise to be back for more, and all while insulting his pride and stamina in the same breath.

"Jesus, Mary, and Joseph. It's seven in the morning!" his uncle roared as he stumbled into the kitchen and ripped the plug of the coffee grinder out of the wall.

"Yo, Ian. I told you I needed to take the car in this morning." Mac plugged the grinder back in and finished grinding the beans. Then he started the coffee pot and brooded.

"I thought you meant later in the day." Ian frowned. "So the invite to spend the night wasn't for some early morning bonding. Thank God."

Mac thought it funny people often thought of them as father and son. Especially since Mac took after him, or so he'd been told. Ian looked years younger than fifty-five. He lifted and ran like a maniac, a former Marine and proud of it. Like Mac, he took stock in action, not words. Ian had never hurt for female companionship, Julie's betrayal notwithstanding. Mac loved the arrogant bastard, and he'd never forgotten how Ian had changed his life to take in his wayward nephew.

But Mac still liked aggravating the man. "Sorry, Uncle Ian. I forget you old people need your rest."

"Fuck off." Ian grumbled as he slammed through cupboards before finding a mug. He interrupted the coffee flow to pour himself a cup, then sat down and glared at Mac.

"So where were you Friday night? You still haven't said. Geo and I had planned on pizza night."

"I had a date." With the most annoying woman to walk the face of the planet. But that ass... Shit. He wanted another shot at her. At *it*—her ass. Just a body part. Lusting after Maggie didn't mean he thought of the blond as more than a sexual companion.

"Well?"

"Well what?" Mac asked, irritated with the third degree.

Ian's eyes narrowed. "Don't get that tone with me."

"Hey, you told me fuck off."

"I raised you. I can tell you to eat shit, and you should say, 'Yes, Sir,' and get busy spooning it up."

Mac grimaced. "Please. I haven't eaten breakfast yet."

"Pussy."

Mac grinned. "Nice mouth."

"Yeah, yeah." Ian guzzled his coffee. "So who's the lucky lady?"

"Some chick. No one special." He didn't want his uncle nosing into his affairs. The big mouth had taken to training Geo, Shane's younger brother, who had a huge crush on Maggie as it was. Geo would find out about Mac and Maggie, and he'd no doubt tell Shane Mac was "boning" her. Then Shane would pressure Mac to go easy on her tender sensibilities while pulling him into romantic double dates and couples crap.

Mac should go easy? Hadn't he told Shelby that Maggie might be the one to break his heart? Not that he had a heart to break, but she'd kicked his ass out after he'd given the woman orgasms. Who the hell did she think she was?

"Oh yeah. Woman problems." Ian chuckled. "The silence is telling. I'd like to meet this one."

"She's nobody. Now how about you get your senile ass

into the shower so I can get a ride to the gym? And hey, make a decision, would you? Are you in or out? You want me running the gym or not, because I need to make plans."

Mac itched to move on. He'd been working at the gym, in limbo for the past two years, while his knee recovered and he settled into civilian life. No longer a part of the Corps, he nevertheless felt a need to surround himself with discipline and order. He'd been filling his uncle's shoes at Jameson's Gym while Ian resolved some investments and business decisions. But Mac was tired of waiting on his life. Being dissed by Maggie only made it worse. He'd waited on her ass long enough. Now he planned on showing her how to behave with her master. Time to take back control of everything.

Ian sighed. "Boy, I'm not sure of anything. I finished up with New York. I'm officially consolidated. But the gym… You're doing a fine job. Why not keep on as you've been?"

"So you can putter around on vacation while I do all the hard work?" Mac snorted, well aware of his uncle's antics. "Please. You're paying me less than a temp's wages, and I'm not even getting vacation time."

"You're getting pussy," Ian said bluntly. "You should be thanking me."

"Nice." He scowled. Maggie was more than pussy. Aggravating, cute, sweet, and demonic. A woman with issues, because no one ever told Mac to leave. It was always the other way around. Always. Without fail. Until now.

"Anyway," Ian continued. "After I drop you off today, I have plans. So you'll need to get a ride home."

Mac sighed. "I guess we're done talking about my future. I'll just keep trudging away while my family takes advantage."

Instead of feeling bad, Ian stood and slapped him on the back hard enough to make him choke. The bastard had a mean right, and he'd never been intimidated by Mac. "Good boy. Now make me some eggs while I shower. And don't burn them."

After Ian left, Mac swore as he slaved over the stove. Ian wouldn't appreciate the touch of curry or hint of parmesan in the eggs. He wouldn't thank Mac for the added bacon and toast. An image of Maggie moaning over Mac's stir fry suddenly came to mind.

"Maybe I should cook for her again before I spank the crap out of her. Quick on the draw my ass." He slammed a few pans together while he finished his uncle's breakfast, determined to show the woman who was boss, once and for all.

Ian watched his nephew banging pots with fascination. Definitely woman problems. Geo had been picking his brain Friday night. The high school senior had a bright future ahead of him. The boy was popular with the ladies, had a few leads on football scholarships and a giant brain to match his ego. A great kid who reminded Ian a lot of Mac. Or the way Mac used to be.

He frowned and wondered if he'd been to blame for his nephew's change. Mac had been a steady kid, not taking after his loser of a mother or troubled father. As much as Ian had loved his brother Brian, Brian hadn't been strong enough to handle Marissa. When Brian had died, Marissa had left without looking back, leaving Ian with an eight-year-old and no way to care for him except to leave the Corps and start over.

At the time, Ian had thought his life had ended. Instead, it had just begun. He loved Mac to death, but the stubborn bastard couldn't see past Ian's mistakes to a bright future of his own.

Mac refused to commit to a woman, and if anyone needed an honest relationship, it was Mackenzie Jameson. The boy had been left too many times by those he loved. First Marissa, then Brian. He'd formed a tight bond with Julie, Ian's biggest mistake and regrettable heartache. He'd poured his heart and soul into the woman. Unfortunately, so had Mac.

When Julie had left him, it had hurt. He knew he was partly to blame, but she hadn't wanted to give them a chance. And she left not only him, but Mac as well. The boy hadn't taken it well at all. Julie had acted as his mother for four long years before she'd fucked Ian over and split.

Still a kid, just a twelve-year-old wanting a mother's love, Mac had lashed out. But the rebellion hadn't lasted, and Ian soon had his hands full of a scholar athlete with too much passion to succeed. A good enough problem to have, except Mac kept a lid on his emotions. On the outside, he excelled. But on the inside, he'd never gotten past the lonely little boy fearing rejection.

He went through relationships like most people went through tissues. Never a handful, but one at a time, one after the other. Mac never got angry or hurt over his breakups, because the idiot never let himself care. Until now. He'd certainly never cursed and banged cookware over a woman before.

Ian heard the name "Maggie" and suddenly understood so much more. Ah. Mac had a thing for the pretty little blond working at the gym. The man who didn't get involved seemed awfully annoyed with a woman he refused to talk about.

A good sign. Ian made some noise before entering the kitchen once more. "Where the hell are my eggs?" He watched Mac take hold of his temper and settle down—on the outside.

Mac gripped the spatula with a fist the size of a brick. "Here." He slid the plate across the kitchen island, and Ian caught it before it could go over onto the floor. "Don't choke on them."

"Lovely. Thanks, Mackenzie."

Mac gritted his teeth. The boy hated to be called by his first name. His mother had picked it out. Ian liked to use it to remind Mac to overcome the past and learn from it. *What didn't kill you made you stronger.* An idiom the Marine Corps enforced.

"You're welcome, Ian." Mac took a deep breath and let it out slowly. "Now could we please get a move on? I have to drop off the car in half an hour."

"Aye, aye, Top." Top, a nickname for Mac's last held rank in the Corps—Master Sergeant.

Mac sighed. "It's gonna be a long fuckin' day. I can feel it."

"Right as rain." Ian shoveled some damn fine eggs into his mouth and said around them, "What the hell did you put in this? Tastes like shit."

Mac beat his head against a cabinet, and Ian chuckled. Yep. Time to see a few friends and study the woman who had his nephew's dick in a knot. Then a plan to make sure Mac stayed frustrated, annoyed, and connected to the woman. With any luck, Maggie might very well be the key to unlocking Mac's heart.

Ian grimaced. That sappy shit had to come from a woman, because no way in hell could Ian handle another one of those "open yourself to love" talks he'd once had with the boy so many years ago. He shivered and pushed the plate away. "Well, Top. Let's hit it." He followed Mac's car, plotting on his way to the dealership.

CHAPTER NINE

MAGGIE WIPED THE SWEAT OFF HER FACE WITH A TOWEL and smiled her goodbyes to the group leaving the workout studio. All in all, she'd had a stellar few days. She'd finished all but one of her paper sculptures for Kim and had been working out like a mad woman for Mac. Her added income would help with the Christmas shopping she planned to nail tomorrow. One shot shopping.

Her list had grown considerably from last year. She had her brother, Shelby, Mimi and Ron, and now Shane. Maggie glanced through the glass wall of the workout room and spied Mac laughing with two other guys by the free weights. She couldn't decide whether to get him something or not. She wanted to but she feared he might take her gift the wrong way. He was her boss, they'd been lovers—hell, she'd called him *Master* and liked it—but she wanted them to remain casual friends. The thought of a relationship excited her way too much, so she quashed the idea before she could act on it.

Imagining herself crying over Mac the way she'd cried over too many exes reinforced her notion to stay away. They'd have sex again, because they both wanted the physical gratification, but the emotional thing scared her. She wasn't ready to go down that road again.

"Well, well. If it isn't my favorite aerobics instructor."

She turned to blink up at George Collins, Shane's younger brother. She smiled with true affection. "Geo. How have you been?" She accepted his bear hug and wheezed. "A little tight."

"Oh. Sorry." He let her go, then studied her from head to toe wearing the same smile his older brother wore when looking at Shelby.

Maggie gripped the ends of the towel to cover her breasts. The kid was seventeen, for God's sake. "You know, staring at a woman's breasts is not considered a form of flattery."

"It is in high school." He winked at her. "Besides, I'm no lecher. I think you're beautiful. You need someone who truly appreciates you."

"Oh?" Maggie decided to play. "And what exactly can you do for me that men my age can't?"

Apparently the opening he'd been waiting for. "Great question." Geo led her toward the bench where she'd stashed her gear and fetched her water bottle for her. "I'd take care of you. I mean, those older guys, they don't have any stamina."

She choked on her water. *Please tell me he's not talking about sex.*

"You'd maybe get a dinner out of them, but they'd fall asleep before you hit the end of a movie afterward." Geo made a face. "Shane can barely work ten hours then stay up for poker night. And now that he's with Shelby, he's always tired."

Maggie stifled a grin. "Oh?"

"Yeah. He never wants to go out anymore. Always needing his sleep at night. Guy is like a thirty-two year old Boy Scout. It's embarrassing to the Collins name."

110

Shane wants to sleep with Shelby, more like. She cleared her throat. "That's too bad."

"Then you have guys like Brent, Tom and Mac." Geo pointed at the three of them still talking by the weights. "I mean, sure, they'd do you. No question. But after that first time, it's all downhill. Men peak at eighteen. Heard it in biology class."

"Wonderful what they're teaching you in school."

He grinned. He had the same dark hair and green eyes as Shane. He'd be a lady killer in no time, especially since he had charm all but tattooed to his forehead.

"You know, Geo. You should give Mac lessons in how to deal with women. I think you're on to something."

Geo brightened. "That's what I've been telling him. But Mr. I'm-God's-Gift-to-Women doesn't think so."

She laughed with Geo. Especially when they noticed Mac look over at them and frown.

"What's this?" A deep voice with a slight brogue preceded Ian, Mac's uncle. Another charmer who would have been hell to deal with in his day. Even now she felt like she had to keep on her toes around the older man.

"Hey Ian." Geo took the hardy slap on the back from Mac's uncle with fortitude. "You know Maggie, right?"

"Of course. How are things, Maggie?" Ian smiled at her, and Maggie saw Mac in that broad grin.

Wow. They sure made the Jamesons F-I-N-E fine. Black Irish and built like tanks. If Mac would be like this in another twenty years, she wondered what kept her from signing up. "Things are good," she hastened to say, aware she'd been staring. She fought a blush when Ian gave her a more subtle onceover than Geo's scrutiny. "How are you, Mr. Jameson?"

"Ian, girl. Call me Ian." He sighed. "Things are well

enough, I suppose." He threw an arm around Geo. "With Christmas only a few days away, I confess I'm much behind on my shopping."

"Not me. I finished last week." Geo shook his head. "You can't wait until the last minute or all the good stuff is gone. Besides that, Mom lets me take a day off school to do my shopping. If I wait, I lose the free time with Christmas vacation." Geo smiled. "And I'm not stupid."

"No, you're a smart one. Unlike my stubborn nephew. Boy still hasn't gotten his shit—er, stuff—together. I know he hasn't gotten me that ratchet set I've been wanting, and I all but put the coupon for it in front of his face."

Maggie grinned. "He's a little clueless, isn't he?"

"You can say that again." Geo scoffed. "Guy turned down Megan and Wendy again today. I mean, how often does he think he's gonna get a shot at, uh…" He flushed and looked away from Maggie. "I mean, he doesn't seem to be dating lately. Shane thinks it's a woman. I think he's in a midlife crisis."

"You think?" Ian asked, but his gaze on Maggie warned her to tread warily.

Uh oh. "You could be right. He's forty, isn't he?"

Geo shrugged. "Thirty, forty, he's old."

Ian glared at him. "The boy is thirty-six. Forty isn't old. Neither is sixty, for that matter."

"Sorry, old man. Truth hurts. Suck it up."

Ian snorted. "You're just like your father and brother. Suck it up, my ass. You need to get through school and sign up, *Lieutenant* Collins."

Geo surprised Maggie when he nodded. "I'm going ROTC through school. Already talked to Dad and Mom about it. And I'm going to be a general. That way I'll outrank Shane and

Dad." Geo gave Ian a calculated grin. "And you and Mac too. You guys will have to salute me."

"With pride, boy." Ian ruffled his hair, then put Geo in a headlock.

Maggie watched the play with fascination, not having realized how affectionate Ian would be, considering Mac seemed standoffish unless wanting sex. Then again, that same man had cuddled with her on the couch after offering her a hug. He made her brain hurt trying to figure him out.

"What's that look, Maggie?" Ian asked.

"You seem very different than Mac. He's domineering and standoffish." At work. "But you're...not."

"That's because you're looking at superior genetics." Ian flexed the arm around Geo's neck, and Geo choked. "Oh, sorry. There you go." He let Geo go.

Geo glared at him, fingered his throat, then sighed. "I have to run. Got a date with Andrea." He looked at the clock overhead. "And it's already seven. Later, Ian. See you at Shelby's party, Maggie. Merry Christmas!" He took off like a shot.

"I'd love to have half his energy," Ian said with a groan. He turned a speculative glance back on her. "So what are you up to this holiday season? Got plans? Family, boyfriend? The boy said you'd be at Shelby's party?"

A bit intrusive, but he was her boss, technically. "I usually spend the holidays with Shelby and her family, which this year includes Shane."

"That sounds nice. Shane's a good man, and from what I've heard about Shelby, she seems like a good fit. Mac likes her well enough, and she's done wonders for his knee." Ian looked through the glass at Mac again.

Mac noticed them looking, frowned, and turned back to

his friends.

"Boy is a pain in my ass," Ian muttered.

Mine too.

"But he's family. I love him. We're actually going to Shelby's party as well."

Damn. So much for avoiding Mac at Christmas. Now she'd have to get him a present. She felt better about the fact, because she'd been trying to rationalize why getting him something wouldn't break any of her no-dating rules. "So I'll be seeing you both at Shane's house in a few days. Now if we could just get the sleet and rain to turn to snow, we might get a white Christmas."

"Gotta love the Seattle weather, eh?" They laughed together before Ian noted the clock. "Guess I'd better get going as well. I'd like to say I have a hot date like Geo, but the truth is I have a business appointment."

"This late at night? Bummer."

"Yeah. But some things can't keep. It was nice talking to you, Maggie."

"You too, Ian." She smiled at him, liking the softness in his gaze when he glanced back at Mac. The clear love she heard in his voice for his nephew spoke well of him. As did the remembrance that he'd given up his career to raise Mac. "Mac is lucky to have you."

Ian beamed. "Feel free to remind him of that whenever you like." He left, passing Mac in the doorway.

They exchanged something she couldn't quite make out, then Ian moved away while Mac approached her. "You."

"You." She dragged on sweats over her gym clothes.

"I need a ride home."

She waited with a raised brow. "I need a raise."

"Funny."

"What's the magic word?"

He blew out a breath, and she fought the urge not to laugh. "Would you *please* give me a ride home?"

"Hmm. What's in it for me?" A glance over his shoulder showed Megan pouting as she stared at Mac. Was it wrong that Maggie took joy in the woman's obvious jealousy?

"How about a bonus?"

"What kind of bonus?"

"Drive me home and I'll think of something."

"Please. Drive me home, please."

Mac snarled, "You're on my last friggin' nerve, Doran. So help me, I'm gonna take this out on your ass later."

She shivered and cooed, "Oh, I can't wait." Not smart to bait the tiger, but the flare of interest he couldn't hide made it worth it.

"I am really going to enjoy taming you." He leaned closer to whisper, "Little Sub."

She forced herself not to lean into his heat and took a hasty step back, aware of the glass wall so close. "Yes, well." She coughed and cleared her throat. "That's not appropriate here."

"Why?" He smirked. "Going to claim sexual harassment?"

"No. But I'd think you'd be embarrassed to walk around with a hard-on." She smirked back at him and added in a whisper, "Because when I remind you that I know what you taste like and what you feel like in my snug ass and tight, wet pussy, you'll be thinking about what we did and how hard it made you." The sudden bulge at his shorts showed her she'd improved her dirty talk.

He sat on the bench and lowered his head in his hands, leaning over his lap and effectively hiding his arousal. "Enough, you little witch." He chuckled, surprising her. "Would you wait for me in my office for a minute? I'll walk you out… as soon as I'm able."

She snickered and left. On the way to his office, she passed several of his fan girls.

"Oh my God. What did Mac say to you?" Megan asked. "Did he mention me?"

Maggie wanted to hate the woman, but the pathetic need in her eyes stopped her. Maggie had been there, so wrapped up in a man she couldn't see straight. And then, inevitably, she'd suffer disappointment. "He was talking about the holiday schedule. Sorry, no mention of anyone but his uncle and staff."

Megan frowned. "He looked upset after talking to you."

"Probably." Inspiration struck. A bonus indeed. "I have plans on Christmas Eve and the week after. He's having a hard time filling the slot. Know anyone who could help?"

Megan perked up. "Oh. Maybe I could step in. See you." The woman raced around Maggie back toward the aerobics room.

Maggie would have felt bad about siccing Megan on Mac except she knew he had no interest in her. Hearing Geo talk about Mac turning women down had pleased Maggie to no end. He hadn't lied about that, at least. He'd stated plainly that he only dated one woman at a time. He'd had sex with her, so that might not qualify as a date. But he didn't seem to be having sex with anyone other than her. And though he didn't seem that pleased to see her lately, he acted annoyed with everyone in general, so she didn't take it personally.

A typical Mac mood consisted of grunts, a few growls, and orders. He saved his smiles for the gym patrons. A good thing, because if he smiled at her, she might break down and beg him to continue what they'd started Friday night. Despite wanting to keep her heart safe, she couldn't stop thinking about Mac,

116

what he was doing, how he felt, if he thought about her.

God, now I sound like Megan. It's just great sex. Snap out of it. She'd have an easier time believing that if she hadn't seen him looking at her the last few days with a strange expression on his face. Almost like frustration and longing, which made little sense. The guy constantly had women all over him. Maggie didn't need a man like that. She'd been with boyfriends not half as good looking, and they'd disappointed her time and time again. Mac had easy access to any woman he wanted. Why should Maggie expose herself to trouble she didn't need?

As she made her way to his office and waited, she continued to force herself to look at him with detachment. He was funny and charming when he wanted to be. So what? He had a big cock and knew how to use it. The ability to turn her on and keep her revved during sex more than satisfied her. Why complicate things with a relationship, one he hadn't even asked for? *Typical Maggie.*

She entered his office and closed the door behind her. He wasn't around, so she sat in his big chair and kicked her feet up on his desk. She closed her eyes and concentrated on not liking him more than she had to. Who knew Mac Jameson would be so hard to deny?

♥

Out in the main gym lobby, Ian stood with his hands in his pockets and stared out at the dark, wet night. He had a chill in his bones but a spark in his brain. He hadn't missed how Maggie had looked at Mac, or how his nephew had studied Maggie like he was starving for her.

Ian couldn't blame him. Maggie had outward beauty, no doubt. Petite but curved in all the right places. That light blond hair and blue eyes, her milky skin over clearly defined muscle packed a knockout punch, and then hearing her soft voice and watching her interact with others… She had charm, personality, and a giving heart—exactly what Mac needed.

Seeing her with Geo had reminded him about the last time someone had interfered in a man's personal life. Geo had filled Ian in on the gory details of his lame matchmaking attempts between Shane and Shelby.

Yet the pair seemed tighter than ever. If not for Geo's, Mac's and Shelby's parents' involvement, Shelby might still be languishing as a single woman without love on the horizon.

Ian just had to figure out how to get his nephew on board the love train. He grinned at the thought of it.

"My, my. They do make them handsome out here, don't they?"

He turned to see a gorgeous creature in a fuchsia workout getup so bright he feared his retinas had been scarred. A mature woman with dark red hair frosted with white, merry green eyes, and rings on all her fingers, smiled at him.

He had a hard time breathing. Magnificent didn't come close to describing her. The woman had presence, something he hadn't come across in years. "And who might you be?" he asked, unable to disguise his interest.

"Oh my God. That accent. I think I'm in love." She stepped closer and held out a hand. "I'm Mimi Vanzant. A friend of Maggie's. She's an instructor here."

He knew that name, Vanzant. Ian took her hand and brought it to his lips. "A pleasure."

She flushed and withdrew her hand, but if anything she stepped closer. "Mine as well."

"So you're here to see Maggie, eh?"

"I am. You know her?"

He realized he hadn't introduced himself. "Ian Jameson. You might know Mac, my nephew." Pieces connected in his mind, and he understood fate had dropped this woman in his lap. "You're Shelby's mother, aren't you?" The same woman who'd interfered in her daughter's life and snagged her a man. Ian's grin broadened when she nodded. "Mimi, why don't I treat you to dinner, and we can talk. I've got a problem I think you're more than qualified to help me with."

She stared at him with wide eyes. "Really?"

Realizing she might have mistaken his intent, he hurried to reassure her. "Strictly a platonic dinner. I have a nephew who could use some help. Like the kind you gave Shelby and Shane."

Mimi nodded. "Sounds right up my alley."

Ian had to add, "And after that, well, I'd like to take you out on the town. Been a while since I've had such a striking woman on my arm." He intensified his brogue because she seemed to like it.

Her eyes sparkled. "I don't know how I could refuse such a charming offer from a gentleman." She let him tuck her hand in the crook of his elbow. "Mac's uncle, hmm? I think you and I might already be working toward the same goal. I'm Maggie's spiritual mother, you know."

"You don't say." Ian escorted her to his BMW. After he closed the door after her, he took a deep breath and let it out, reminding himself not to blow this. He was a bit rusty when it came to dating, but it hadn't been so long that he'd forgotten how to handle a woman as sexy as this one. He joined her in the car. "Now where would you like to go, my dear?"

"Hmm. I think I have just the place. It's quiet, the food is good, and if I'm right, we'll need the backup." She took out her phone and called someone named Ron. After she gave him directions, she sat back and sighed. "This car is wonderful. I love the smell of leather."

"Me too." He paused. "So that Ron. Not your boyfriend, is he?"

She laughed, rich, honest amusement she didn't try to cage. He liked her more already. "Ron is my business partner and best friend. We're going to his and his boyfriend's new apartment for dinner and some planning. Will that work?"

Ian smiled. "Sounds perfect." Her best friend had a boyfriend. Outstanding. Now he had a shot at not only snagging a woman for his nephew, but maybe a girlfriend for himself as well. A glance at her widened his grin. "I think this is the beginning of a beautiful friendship, Mimi."

She rested her hand on his shoulder, and he felt a flare of heat all the way to his toes. "I think you may be right."

CHAPTER TEN

MAGGIE DROPPED MAC OFF AT HIS HOUSE. HE WAVED goodbye without a backwards glance. He hadn't made a move or a suggestive comment the whole way home. No mention of payback or their next Master/sub session either, which irked her.

Okay, so Maggie didn't want a relationship with him. She wouldn't mind the opportunity to turn him down, though. Granted, that might make things between them a bit hairy, but it would reinforce her confidence, letting her know he wanted her.

Instead, she had to wonder if he'd gotten what he wanted out of her after all. Like a few before him, once they had her in bed, they backed off. As if sex was the only thing Maggie had to offer. Of course, most of the guys she'd been with had been less than satisfying. Not that she'd dated that many men, but of the ones she'd had sex with, she could count on one hand the number who had sexually fulfilled her.

So depressing. Then to find a man who not only gave her orgasms, but was into the exact kink she needed? There had to be some way to ensure Mac and she could continue their special *friend*ship. But what if he'd accepted an offer from Megan? Perhaps Maggie had pushed Mac too hard, and he didn't want to deal with her anymore.

Bah. She hated feeling torn over a man. She needed to stop thinking about him anyway. Maggie had shopping to do tomorrow.

She made sure to get a good night's sleep and was raring to go the next day. The clouds had disappeared, leaving the streets awash in melting ice and the glow of a rare December sun. A sure sign Maggie needed to indulge in the positive and embrace her Christmas spirit.

Humming while she readied for her big day, she wasn't prepared to hear a knock on her door. Curious, because she had the day completely free and Shelby knew not to call her, Maggie reached her door and looked through the peephole.

To her surprise, she saw Mac standing outside. Dressed in jeans and a winter coat, the man appeared masculine, sexy, and good enough to eat. She had the experience to back up such a claim, and knowing that brought a flush to her cheeks. She calmed herself and straightened her hair before opening the door.

"Mac."

"Hey, Maggie." He pushed past her and headed toward her coffee pot.

"Hey, yourself." She closed the door before following him. "Gee, Mac. Why don't you come on in?" Yet she couldn't deny she liked seeing him in her apartment.

"Thanks." He winked at her, and her heart raced.

"So."

"So." He grabbed her coffee and took a large sip out of it. "Ech. Too sweet. But man, I needed the jolt."

Sighing, she found a clean mug and handed it to him.

He smiled, and after pouring himself a huge helping, finally explained what the hell he was doing there. "I have a favor to ask."

"Another one?"

"So after you drop me off at the car dealer —"

"Excuse me?"

"I need you to pick me up something for Shelby. Something girlie, but not too personal because I don't want Shane on my ass."

"Huh?"

"You're going Christmas shopping today, right? You bitched about not having any time so much that it made my ears bleed."

"Jackass."

"So will you do it?"

"Why don't you shop for her? It's the thought that counts, right?"

He groaned. "Women. You tell men you want us to think of something, and when we do, it's wrong." He narrowed his gaze. "Take you for instance."

"What about me?" She put her hands on her hips, annoyed. "I haven't asked you for anything."

"Besides a spanking," he murmured before quickly following with, "if I were to get you something for Christmas, I'd buy you a pretty teddy. Some lace panties, maybe some edible body butter."

"For Christmas? Who is this for, you or me?"

"See? I thought you'd be this way." Yet his smile told her he'd intended to rile her. "So use your taste to buy Shelby something she'd like. What do you want for Christmas? Think along those lines. So what are we talking? Books, lingerie, perfume?"

"Is this your pathetic way to see what I want for Christmas?"

"Nope. I just know you and Shelby think alike."

"Well, that's true." She thought about it. "I don't know. Candles, soaps. Some perfume, but you have to get the right kind. Perfume is kind of like shoes. Everyone has a certain taste."

"See? I'd be wrong already. So no chain and collar, eh?"

She tamped down the excitement at the idea. "And no on the nipple clamps," she added drily.

He made a sad face, and she laughed.

"Okay. I'll pick something up for her for you. But you're wrapping it."

"Awesome." He dug in his pocket and handed her a hundred dollars, cash.

How nice to be able to spend that much on your friend's girlfriend. She stifled a sigh. She'd saved all year long to make her Christmas budget and still afford her bills. The year hadn't been that bad, and her overtime at the gallery and extra gym hours helped. But still...

She pocketed the money. "Anything else, moneybags?"

"Yeah, this." He kissed her on the cheek.

The cheek.

"Thanks for doing this, Maggie. I owe you." He finished his coffee, put his cup in the sink, then grabbed her keys off the counter. "So you ready to go or what?"

Or what, she thought half an hour later. Mac Jameson had kissed her friggin' cheek. That bastard. No sexual innuendo, no groping, and no hints about more spankings. What the hell was he thinking?

She stewed about him most of the morning as she bought

Shelby a few purchases with his money. But as the day progressed, she put him out of her mind and threw herself into the Christmas spirit. The day was too fine not to enjoy peppermint cocoa, carolers downtown, and her barrage of gifts. She couldn't wait to see Mimi's face when Maggie gave her more bangles to add to her collection. Or Ron's face when she gave him the special tea he liked—the stuff was rare, expensive, and almost impossible to find, even in Seattle. For Shelby she'd found a cashmere sweater that cost a pretty penny, and for Shane a framed picture of him and Shelby that Maggie had had professionally mounted.

For Trevor she'd bought a collection of anime her weirdo older brother loved, as well as a new wool scarf and gloves, because more than likely he'd lost the last pair she'd given him. The man was forever losing hats too, so she'd added that to her list. She'd keep it all wrapped so that when he returned in the spring, they could have a belated holiday together.

She had everyone done... almost. Mac. She didn't know what to give him. The man seemed to be interested in fitness, the Marine Corps, and women. He worked at a gym, had all the Marine stuff he could want, and she had no intention of hooking him up with anyone but herself.

An idea sparked, and she headed to a few stores she'd seen but had never had the courage to enter before now. A corset, fuzzy heels, a collar and chain later, she left the downtown area with her purchases. She felt warm all over, not having had this much fun in a long while.

Later that evening, her phone rang. Mac's number. All at once, his dismissal from that morning came rushing back, and she felt like an idiot for blowing so much on sexy clothes. Especially when he asked for yet *another* favor.

"Hey Maggie. Could you pick me up at the car dealer? My

uncle left me here, and my car isn't ready yet. Shane's busy, and I can't get a hold of Shelby either."

"Call a cab," she said flatly, all her Christmas cheer gone in the space of one phone call.

"I guess I could call Megan. She gave me her number. Sorry for bothering you. I'll—"

"Damn it. I'll be there in twenty minutes." She hung up before he could change his mind. Megan? He'd call that floozy? More to the point, why did he have Megan's number on hand? It was one thing to take her number and stash it somewhere, but to have it on his phone? On his person?

She stewed on her drive to pick him up, and after getting him, continued to brood all the way to his place.

While he talked about what a productive day he'd had at work, she remained silent.

"Hey, you okay?" Mac tapped her leg, and the traitorous limb wanted to leap at the contact.

She forced a smile. "Fine. Just tired. I did a lot of shopping today." *Shopping for you, you big jackass.*

"Oh, right. Was the money enough?"

He had no right looking so concerned, so masculine and commanding and…

"It was enough." She hated that she sounded hoarse.

He smiled. "Good. So you're done with your shopping? Nice. I still have Ian to get to."

"Is it Ian or Uncle Ian?"

"Either. Man answers to most things I call him." Mac chuckled. "But he doesn't take any shit, that's for sure. Swears up and down, but God forbid I tell him off when he's earned it. Man has control issues."

She parked the car in front of his house. "You did not just say that. *He* has control issues?"

He shrugged. "I get it honestly, don't I?"

How would I know? It's been forever since I've experienced my master, she wanted to say but didn't. Instead she waited with a brittle smile.

Mac paused. "Despite ordering you around all the time at the gym, I feel bad about doing it on your day off."

That surprised her.

"Would you mind coming in for a minute more? I swear I won't take up the rest of your night. You probably have plans."

"Yeah. It's a Wonderful Life is on TV tonight." And a bottle of wine sat in the fridge. She should have felt happy about having so little to do for once. She could enjoy herself without guilt. Her last project to hand over to Kim had nearly finished drying. Maggie would have it done in a few hours at most. But instead of looking forward to her night, she felt lonely. Shelby had Shane. Trevor had his work only God knew where, which seemed to satisfy him. Mac had his uncle. Who did Maggie have?

"Can you give me your opinion on something I got for Shane's mom?"

She hadn't thought about the other women in Mac's life, but she'd heard from Shane how tight Mac was with his family. "Sure." It couldn't hurt, and she had no rush to return to an empty home.

After turning off the car, she got out and locked it up, conscious of her many gifts in the trunk. She followed Mac inside and sighed at the warmth that eased her frozen fingers. Her gloves seriously needed replacing.

"Cold out today," Mac's low voice helped warm her up.

"Yeah. It's a wet cold. I hate that."

"No kidding. Ian's always grumbling about his bones aching." Mac took off his shoes and coat, then hung the jacket in the closet. He turned to her and removed her jacket before she could ask what the hell he was doing. "Habit, sorry."

"What, stripping your visitors without asking?"

"Being neat about it. You don't need a coat in here. I pay the heat bills." He grinned at her, and she wanted to slap him for losing interest in her so quickly. Why was it he looked more handsome today? Because he wasn't available anymore? God, she was such an idiot when it came to men.

"The gift is upstairs. No etchings, I promise."

She snorted. "Yeah, right. You, etchings? I see nothing but photography on the walls. Not that they aren't pretty, but you could vary the pictures a little." After toeing off her shoes and leaving them by the front door, she followed him up the stairs.

She hadn't seen this part of his home before. The walls had a tan wash, white baseboards and trim that accentuated the brown. It felt warm and inviting, masculine without being too overbearing. She passed two bedrooms and a bath before coming to his bedroom.

"This is it. Where all the magic happens." He wiggled his brows.

God, the man had been nothing but charming all day. He annoyed the crap out of her.

"Yeah, yeah." She entered, shocked to actually like his style. A dark blue wall brought focus to the king-size poster bed. "Well, that fits you. A big bed for your big ego."

He chuckled. "Aren't you cute?"

She blew out a breath. He wouldn't even take the bait. So depressing. Maggie looked around, spotting a mahogany dresser and mirror facing the bed, an armoire, and a big leather chair in the corner, which would be a perfect spot for reading if the Neanderthal in front of her knew how to crack a book.

"Nice, huh?"

He seemed to be waiting for her approval.

"It suits you."

He nodded. "It does. The present is over here." He pointed to the nightstand.

She frowned. "You're giving Shane's mom furniture?"

"What? No, that box."

She saw the small box, what looked like a jeweler's box. A nice gift. Curious, she went to the stand and picked up the box. When she opened it, she saw a slender chain with two funny looking ends. Some kind of weird necklace, maybe?

Before she could ask him what it was, Mac wrapped his arms around her, hugging her into his aroused frame.

Shocked, because he'd been anything but sexually aware of her, or so it had seemed, she struggled.

"Now, now. You were a naughty sub, weren't you? And yesterday, getting me all hot and bothered in the gym? Did you really think you wouldn't get punished?"

Oh, God. He wants me.

Mac ground against her ass, and Maggie turned immediately wet. Joy infused her as Mac sucked hard on her neck, enough to leave a mark.

His next action stunned her. With rough hands, he stripped her naked and shoved her onto her back on the bed. She froze, wondering what he'd do next. He tied her up to the posts, securing her enough that she couldn't move. Splayed out like a human X, naked, vulnerable, and completely turned on.

"That's pretty." He cocked his head and studied her. "But not right, not yet." He leaned down and sucked both her nipples, first the left, then the right, until they stood on end. "That's better." He grabbed the jewelry box from the nightstand and removed the chain.

Realization dawned, as did a fresh surge of excitement.

Marie Harte

"Nipple clamps? You lied to me about that present."

He grunted. "No shit. You're so easy."

"Up yours." The minute she said it, she knew she'd made a mistake. And she creamed like crazy.

His mean smile made her groan. "We're going to have a lot of fun tonight, little sub."

"But, Sir, I didn't mean—"

"The hell you didn't. You've been mouthing off and teasing me for days. You think I don't know how much you need this?" He shoved a finger inside her, and she bucked into his touch. "How much you need *me*?"

He withdrew his finger and licked it. "Hmm. You taste hungry. You missed me, didn't you?"

"Yes, Sir." She felt like sobbing. She'd missed the hell out of him despite trying to remain distant. To her dismay, his disinterest had hurt more than she might have imagined.

He took off his shirt but nothing else. His jeans had a familiar bulge, his long, thick cock trapped beneath the denim. She wanted to feel him inside her again, but more, she wanted him to order her around. To kneel, to crawl, to take him any and every way *he* wanted. She was such a freak.

"Why that look? Tell me what you're thinking. Don't lie to me."

She blinked away useless tears. "I want to serve you, Sir. And that's just not normal."

The angry expression on his face softened. "No. That's normal for people like us, Maggie. Tell me what you want me to do."

"I... I want..."

"Tell me." He stroked her breasts and belly, petting and caressing as he angled toward her mound. There he played with her labia, sliding his fingers perilously close to her clit but

130

staying maddeningly distanced.

"Please, Sir." She wriggled her hips, nearly undone. Tied up and helpless, her master touching her. She *loved* this. "I don't want to tell you anything. I want you to tell me what to do. All of it. Punish me. Discipline me. Fuck me." *Love me.*

"Ah, you need it bad, don't you? Some hard fucking." He pinched her clit, and she arched up into the blaze of desire, hovering on the brink of orgasm. Then he let her go. "Good girl. You don't come unless I tell you to. Understand?"

She nodded. "Yes, Sir."

"Good." Mac leaned down to kiss her nipples again, but this time when he finished, he set one of the clamps on her.

The pain was explosive. She cried out even as her womb clenched. God, that turned her on. She'd never thought her nipples would be so sensitive. Mac set the other on her, and he praised her when she accepted it as well.

"That's nice. Oh yeah." He tugged on the slender gold chain holding the clips together. The pressure on her nipples hurt yet warmed, shocking a gasp out of her. "That pussy is so wet. You're dripping on my sheets."

She flushed, completely embarrassed.

Mac shook his head, his eyes so dark they looked black. He seemed like an avenging conqueror looming close, his broad chest and huge muscles a challenge to glance away from. "No discipline. It's a good thing Master is here to help you, isn't it, sub?" He unzipped his fly and pulled his thick cock out.

"Yes, Sir," she moaned and licked her lips, wanting to suck him dry. He left only his cock exposed, so she couldn't see his balls or anything but his shaft. That sexy tease made her hunger worse.

"Hmm. Where should I put this, I wonder?" He held himself for her, and she loved the sight of fluid at his tip. He wanted her just as much as she wanted him. "How about I slide between those tits?"

Mac knelt on the bed and leaned down. He pressed her breasts together and rubbed against the chain when he slid forward. She hissed at the drag on her nipples. He had to be in pain as well, because he grazed the chain against his sensitive flesh. But Mac's breathing grew heavier as he slowly slid back and forth between her breasts.

"Do you like this?"

"Yes, Sir. Very much."

"But I bet you're like to suck my cock, wouldn't you?" He thrust through her breasts and pushed at her lips, where he held fast.

She wanted to suck him in, but he hadn't given her permission.

"Good girl. Very good." He reached behind him and rubbed her slick clit. She opened her mouth on a gasp and he inched between her lips. "Tricky little sub. Get Master all excited with your big tits and your wet pussy. Why don't you suck me?"

She moaned her assent and sucked his thick cockhead, wiping his slit with her tongue. He continued to play with her pussy while he pumped just the head of himself into her mouth, and the teasing drove her to distraction. She needed to come, but more, she wanted to please her master. Mac became her whole world as she centered her concentration on him.

"Oh, fuck. That's so good." He pushed more of himself into her, touching the roof of her mouth. "You make me forget myself. How much I have to spank you before fucking the brat out of you," he whispered while shoving farther into her. He removed his fingers from between her legs and angled himself so that he could fuck her mouth. "Open wider, little sub."

She did, and he pushed hard and fast to the back of her throat.

She choked while he held himself there. But her spasm left her, making it hard to breathe. The pleasure of holding him in her mouth transformed her discomfort into all consuming pleasure.

Mac withdrew and stared down at her, nodding. "That's better. That's the look I want to see on your face."

She didn't know what he meant but agreed anyway. "Yes, Sir."

Mac climbed between her legs and stared down at her thighs. "You're strong, such tone. You're fucking hot as hell in tights. But naked?" He knelt down and put his mouth on level with her clit. "Time to see how sweet you taste."

"Master," she sobbed, needing to come.

He winked at her before sucking her clit into his mouth, and she moaned in ecstatic agony as she fought not to come. The touch of his tongue felt so good, the pain of denying her climax almost hurt.

"That's nice." He played with her folds, spreading her cream over her thighs and down, slicking her perineum toward her ass. "I want in here, to spread you wide. But we need more lube. Come for me. All over my tongue." He licked her and sucked her clit hard, ramping her tension once more.

The painful pleasure overwhelmed her. He reached to tug the chain between her breasts and sucked harder while he pulled.

A rush of desire stole her breath, and Maggie screamed as she came harder than she ever had. The orgasm pulsed through her, robbing her breath, her will, her desire for anything other than Mac.

"God, you're so fucking hot when you come." Mac pulled

up from between her legs and released the chain. He stripped out of the rest of his clothes and reached into his bedside drawer, where he withdrew a tube of lubricant. He smeared it over his engorged cock and watched her.

"Now, little sub. Time for the rest of your punishment."

CHAPTER ELEVEN

MAC DIDN'T KNOW HOW HE'D LASTED THIS LONG. Knowing how annoyed she'd been earlier had salved the ego she'd pricked days ago. So she thought he'd come too fast, had she? He'd taken his time getting back with her, stretching out the anticipation.

He'd wanted to laugh at her disappointment when he'd kissed her on the cheek. The little liar wore her emotions on her sleeve, and he knew she'd expected an assault on her senses. *Only on my timetable, Maggie. You're mine now, and it's time to hammer that home.*

The dichotomy of the woman chained up under him and the termagant who refused to obey him at the gym pleased the hell out of him. Maggie didn't have it in her to bow to him all the time. She liked tell him what to do and where to go, but she loved his mastery in bed. The perfect woman, as far as he was concerned.

And that worried him. He hadn't liked her talking to Ian and Geo at the gym. He wanted nothing to come between him and Maggie. Not until he had a handle on his weird feelings.

Seeing her eyes glaze over as she gave herself fully to him was a thing of beauty, and he knew he'd never forget that. Her acceptance burned into his brain. Even now, limp and open, totally his for the taking, she challenged him to be more, to truly give her what she needed.

Mac knelt between her legs and angled her up to accept him. Her ass was tight, and he didn't like hurting her. But *she* liked it. He'd seen her flinch and heard her sigh the last time. His little blond fairy liked the bite of pain. Hell, she'd soaked his sheets when he'd tugged on that chain.

Fuck if seeing her wearing it didn't make him want to explode. He wanted to come on her tits, on her face. He wanted to watch himself jet onto her tongue and see her swallow him. So sexy, owning this woman's pleasure. But he had to have her now. To reassert his position and make sure she knew her place.

"What's your safe word, Maggie?" he growled as he rested his tip at her anus.

She moaned and closed her eyes, trying to seat him deeper.

"I asked you a question, sub. Open your fucking eyes." He gripped her hips hard, putting his fingertips over the slight bruises left from their last time. Seeing those marks aroused him unbearably.

Maggie blinked up at him and smiled, and damn if his heart didn't flip over in his chest and swan dive at her feet. "Yes, Master."

"Your safe word." He pushed the tip of himself inside her and caught a moan of his own. She parted her full lips and licked her bottom lip.

"Strawberry, Sir," she whispered.

"You use it if you have to," he reminded her as he pushed

the rest of himself through her tight passage. "That's it. Take me, girl. Take Master up that ass."

She squirmed as he pushed all the way in, but lubed as he was, he had a much easier time taking her than the last foray in her bedroom.

"What would make you happy, little sub?" he asked once he'd seated himself balls deep. Christ, she was tight.

"Master. Yes," she hissed when he shifted and ground against her. "Come inside me. Fill me up, please, Sir."

"Yeah." He started fucking her, slowly, so he could watch himself glide in and out of her. She clamped down on him so beautifully, as if she'd been made for him. The pleasure was out of this world. "You feel good, sub. So tight. That's it. Squeeze me as I fuck you. Come hard."

She clenched, and he lost his mind. He pumped faster, at his limit, yet remained conscious of his desire to make it just as good for her. He rubbed her clit and deliberately slowed down, feeling the ecstasy bunch at the base of his spine, fill his balls and travel throughout his body. He was coming hard, but he wanted her with him.

"Yes, Master. Oh God." She tried to rip her hands free from the chains but they held. And watching her fight her restraints, lost in the pleasure, took the last vestiges of his control.

He slammed into her ass, rocking with speed while he rubbed her taut clit harder.

"Yes, yes," she cried. "Sir, *yes.*"

She clamped on him like a vise, and he saw stars behind his eyes as he shot forward and held, pumping into her ass.

"Maggie, oh fuck." He continued to grind her clit, knowing the sensation would only fuel her pleasure, especially when the pain hit.

She jerked and cried out again, and he felt another ripple pass through her.

Mac pulled his hands away but remained inside her. He stared down at his submissive, lost in the cloud of pleasure drugging his being. *This* was what he'd been missing his entire fucking life.

"You okay, Maggie?"

She blinked up at him like a well-fed cat. "Oh, God. That was so good, Sir." The natural way she said that told him she'd embraced his dominance. No pause, no halfhearted *Sir*.

"Who's your master, sub?" he asked softly.

"You, Sir."

"And who are you to me?"

"Your sub, Sir." Maggie smiled, and then that smile faded.

"What's wrong?" He had a feeling he knew. Maggie had gotten off like he had, sensing a connection, having experienced the ultimate in pleasure. And like him, she wanted to run for the hills and not look back. For that reason, he wouldn't let either one of them escape. As scary as it seemed, he refused to cower or leave without seeing this through. Strength lay in discipline, and he decided to embrace their unexpected bond. Their new…*relationship*.

"I like this. A lot." She paused. "I don't want it to end, Sir."

He remained inside her, not willing to give her up. Mac stroked her belly and her breasts, toyed with the clamps and the chain. She bit her lip but said nothing.

"Tell me the truth. You don't like the thought of me with Megan or any of the others."

She scowled, and he hid a grin. His feisty sub excited him still. Even after experiencing the ultimate high, he wanted her again.

"No, Sir. I don't like the thought of you with any of those skanks."

He raised a brow, pleased when she blushed. "Did you miss me these last few days?"

She sounded miserable when she answered, "Yes, Sir."

"Did you mean what you said last time? That I was too fast for you?" That still irked him.

"No, Sir."

"What? I can't hear you." He jerked the chain, and she moaned. He felt a twitch in his balls, a need for more of his little sub.

"No, Sir," Maggie said in a louder voice.

"Then why did you say it?"

She sighed but didn't look away. "To needle you. You're arrogant." She smiled. "Sir."

"True."

Her lips firmed and her eyes watered. "And I wanted you to come back to me again. But I didn't want to ask you to."

"Why not?"

"Because you might say no." A tear slid down her cheek, and Mac felt his heart break along with hers.

"Oh, damn. Maggie, don't cry." He kissed the tear and wiped her cheeks. "Honey, if you can't feel what you do to me, I must not be doing it right."

Her short laugh tensed her body against his, and he sucked in a breath. He started to grow hard again. "This—*us*—we're going to take it day by day, all right?"

"Yes."

"Do you want a relationship?" Funny, but it no longer hurt to say the word.

"N-no, Sir." She didn't seem sure, and he thought he saw longing in her eyes.

He thought about it. Maggie, for all that she was a bombshell, had been hurt in the past. Hell, the woman had been celibate for months in an effort to distance herself from losers. Sure she'd be scared about trying someone new. But Mac wasn't just anyone. He was her master.

"Too bad, little sub. You have one now."

Her eyes widened, and he continued, sure of himself and where this relationship needed to go. For now. Just for now, he told himself. Maybe he could help Maggie see that not all guys were fuckheads while pleasing them both in the process. A win-win.

"I'm your master, and you're my sub. We don't fuck anyone else while we're in this *relationship*. At work and when not in bed, you're you, I'm me. You call me dickhead, asshole, whatever floats your boat." Her slow smile warmed his entire body. "I can't promise not to take charge, because that's who I am. But you'll never be punished for something outside our zone. This, us together like this, Master to sub, that's our zone. And when we're in it, you'll know."

"Are we in it now, Sir?" she asked softly, no longer looking sad, but ecstatic.

"You're damn right we are." He wiggled his hips and grew harder. "You lied to me. You deliberately hurt your master's feelings to manipulate me." And nicely done. She'd had him committed to punishing her without having to expose herself at all. No rejection from him, because she'd goaded him into returning to prove a point. "You're a tricky little sub, but I can handle that."

She could keep up with him. He knew it.

"Yes, Sir." She looked down, but the curl of her lips gave her away.

"You're not upset you hurt your master's feelings?" He

had to work to still his own grin.

"O-of course I am, Sir." She laughed. "Oops. I really am sorry." She shifted, and he slid deeper inside her again.

Mac withdrew and stood, his erection at half mast. "Time to show you who's really boss. I top, not you."

She looked confused, but that was okay. He'd explain it to her one inch at a time.

Maggie stood under the spray and watched Mac out of the corner of her eye. Good Lord, but if the man know how happy she was right now, he'd probably paddle her. He'd been plotting and planning how to manage her for days, when she'd thought he'd tired of her.

Excitement spiraled through her, and she had to remind herself not to look like a kid at Christmas. As he stood there glaring at her, like a Greek god under the spray of water, she averted her gaze and continued to wash him. She loved touching him, and the soap made his skin feel silky, so that running her hands over his arms and chest and belly was like stroking pure pleasure.

"You're a dirty little girl, aren't you?" Mac rasped as she massaged his cock and balls. He was hard, and she got off making him so aroused.

"Yes, Sir."

"You like getting mc worked up, don't you?" He gripped her by the throat, and she moaned.

"Yes, Sir. You're so sexy."

"Hmm."

He stared at her while she masturbated him. His balls had grown hard, his nipples tight, and she knew it was a short matter of time before he came.

He shoved her against the wall of the shower. Mac used

firmness to show his mastery, but he'd never hurt her. That balance of power thrilled her to no end. Next to her, he seemed so big. Massive and powerful, and he wouldn't let her get away with anything.

"You're shaking." Mac sneered at her. "Turn around."

She reluctantly let him go, then gasped as he bent her over and shoved hard into her pussy.

"Bad girl, getting your master all worked up." He fucked her hard from behind, and his excitement intensified her own. "But you don't get to come. Not yet." He pounded a few more times before swearing as he came. "*Fuck*. Shit, that's it. Yeah." He pulled out, turned her around, and pushed her to her knees. "Lick me clean."

She tasted more water than herself around him as she serviced him, but it was the thought of being on her knees, of having to bow to his command, that gave her true pleasure. That and he'd come inside her again. Maggie loved when he did that, when he shared that physical part of himself. If she weren't on birth control, she had a feeling they'd have made a baby. The thought of carrying his child simultaneously delighted and scared her. She was falling hard for Mac with no way out. She didn't know if it was healthy, but she didn't want to stop her rollercoaster of emotions.

"Tsk tsk." He gripped her by the hair and pulled her up to her feet. "Not paying attention to task. More punishment. I swear, it's like you're begging for another spanking."

Maggie moaned.

He laughed. "Man, you're just full of surprises. How about dirty talk? You want me to call you a whore? Want me to put you down and fuck you like the dirty slut you are?" he asked, his voice thick, and kissed her hard.

"Yes, Sir." With anyone else, she wouldn't have had the

courage to ask. No one else had ever offered to fulfill her naughty fantasies. Her need to be bossed around, owned, even denigrated to an extent. Shelby would stare at her in horror if she knew what Maggie desired.

"It's okay, little sub," Mac whispered. "I know what you feel. Is it wrong if I get off calling you a whore while I fuck you? If I like half choking you while I take you?" He stroked her throat instead of holding her. "I like the fantasy. But you need to know I'd never truly hurt you, Maggie. And I for sure don't think you're a slut." He snorted. "It was damn hard getting into your pants in the first place."

She let out a sigh of relief. "I just don't want you to think I'm a pervert or freak or anything."

"Maggie." He kissed her hard and gripped her throat again. "With me, you're safe. I'm your master. Say it."

"You're my master."

He shook his head, and with the water washing down his face, his lashes glistening, his eyes bright and clear and so dear to her, he buried himself in her heart. "Say it like you mean it, little sub. Show Master how much he means to you."

He met her gaze, and as he stared at her, something in his expression seemed to give.

"Show me, baby," he whispered.

She kissed him, so softly it was a whisper of breath between them. And then she continued, caressing him with her mouth, all over his body.

Until he was moaning her name, praising his little sub, and holding her tight as he came, and all through the night.

CHAPTER TWELVE

MAGGIE DIDN'T KNOW HOW IT HAD HAPPENED, BUT somehow, she found every minute of every day accounted for until Christmas. Mimi and Ron, Shelby, and even Shane dominated her free time. Kim had been ecstatic with the rest of her pieces, so at least Maggie had her deadlines covered. But honestly, her friends had become needy for attention lately.

Her time at the gym passed the way it normally did. She and Mac sniped at each other. She felt him watching when she wasn't looking, but no one commented on anything between them. She made sure to treat him the way she always did, with irreverence and an attitude just shy of disrespect. He was the boss, but it didn't help to pander to his ego. She'd seen the many presents he'd received from an assortment of women.

She'd secretly fumed about it, then been more than grateful to receive her own share of candy and flowers from male admirers. Mac hadn't been too happy about that.

They'd spent the past two days apart, and as Christmas Eve dawned, she had her day planned around a morning outing with Shelby and her evening with Mimi and Ron. The actual party would take place at Shane's house on Christmas.

It irked her that her contact with Mac had been limited to texts, but the man wasn't good about answering calls, so she could only do so much. His texts amused her. He abbreviated everything, half of which she barely understood. But from the gist of what she'd read, his uncle, Shane, and Geo were annoying the hell out of him.

She couldn't wait to show him her Christmas presents.

A knock on her door startled her, and she looked at the time. Nine o'clock. Shelby had arrived for their morning together. Maggie opened the door and nearly fell under the massive hug from her giant friend.

"Oomph."

"Merry Christmas!" Shelby danced around, swinging Maggie like a ragdoll.

"Put me down, you freakish giant," Maggie pleaded, laughing at her friend's lunacy.

When Shelby did, Maggie saw a rock on her finger. She glanced at Shelby's beaming face, then looked back at the ring. "That's an engagement ring," she said stupidly. "You got engaged." She blinked, then laughed. "Oh my God. *You got engaged.*" She squealed with joy and hugged Shelby back. "Let me look. Oh wow! He must really love you. That's a friggin' rock."

She and Shelby went out for breakfast to celebrate. Maggie peppered her friend with questions, but Shelby remained surprisingly tight-lipped, her interest in Maggie's life a little strange.

"Seriously?" Maggie stared at her best bud over her coffee cup. The waiter brought their breakfasts then left, and Maggie continued. "You're engaged to be married. You and Shane are actually moving in together, and you have nothing better to talk about than my love life?"

"Um, well, no. I just don't want to be all about me."

"Hey, loser, this *is* all about you. I'm not the one getting married."

"Who are you calling a loser, cat lady?" Shelby's smirk told Maggie to be cautious. "But then, you're not the cat lady anymore, are you?"

"I don't know what you mean." Though Maggie and Mac had agreed to be discreet, it wasn't as if she was embarrassed to be with him. But she didn't know where their relationship might take them, and she didn't want to be pitied when, not if, they broke up. For some reason, Shelby always acted like Maggie should be coddled after a breakup, which made Maggie feel bad. Sometimes relationships ended. Normally, without smothering empathy from her friend, she accepted the termination, half expecting it anyway.

"I can't say for sure, but I get the feeling you've met someone. There's a look in your eye I recognize. But it's different. It's like you're glowing." Shelby paused. "You're not pregnant are you?"

Maggie choked on the coffee she'd been in the process of swallowing. "No, you idiot." At least, she didn't think so.

"Oh my God. You turned red. You're having sex."

"Would you shut up?" Maggie blushed harder when several people near them looked at their table. "First of all, my private life is private. Second, this is not the place to talk about stuff like that. You're turning into your mother."

"Okay, that was just mean." Shelby had been dealing with a flamboyant but well meaning mother her entire life. She didn't like being the center of attention any more than Maggie did. "Can't I be happy for us?"

"No. Be happy for *you*. You're engaged. I might have had a

good night. But until I know if it will go anywhere, I'm keeping quiet." The disappointment on her friend's face forced Maggie to confess, "I think I really like him. And I don't want to see your pity when we break up, okay? So give me a few more days, maybe a week or two, to enjoy him. Then when he and I break off, we can share some ice cream and talk about how men suck."

"Okay." Like that, Shelby let it go.

It was too easy. "I mean it."

"Yeah, yeah." Shelby held out her hand. "So let's talk about my ring."

"Let's."

They spent the rest of the morning laughing and walking around Queen Anne. Maggie liked how excited Shelby was about moving in with Shane. She'd been such a mess for so long that seeing her in love and happy about the engagement was like a balm to Maggie's own hurts. If Shelby could find love with a decent guy, that meant Maggie had hope.

An immediate image of Mac came to mind. She smiled to herself, holding onto that closeness they'd shared. When he'd let her be herself, when he'd accepted the dirty, terrible desires she had and fed them, he'd given her more than a sexual rush, but a deep seated contentment, that maybe she wasn't so bad a person for having weird desires. She wasn't the only one who'd gotten off on the naughty talk, or the spanking, or the anal sex.

She hurried to rejoin Shelby by a chocolate store and wondered if Mac would like the other present she'd decided to give him. The sex he'd love, she had no doubt. But the other item had come straight from her heart. She just hoped he wouldn't laugh at her. No, Mac wouldn't laugh, but if he didn't treasure it like she hoped, he'd hurt a part of herself she'd unconsciously given him.

Marie Harte

Her time with Shelby passed swiftly. Shelby returned to Shane's, breaking up his guy time with Mac, Geo and his father. Apparently the Collins family had decided to fly to Portland to spend the holiday with his mother's relatives, leaving Shane to spend Christmas with Shelby and her family. *Which includes me,* Maggie thought, pleased.

And on that note… She checked her messages for any word from Trevor and frowned, finding none. She knew he had business to take care of, but a nice note to his sister wouldn't have been too much to ask.

Due at Mimi's in another hour, she refreshed her makeup and grabbed gifts for everyone. Then she drove over and parked behind several other vehicles. Mimi lived in a home in Queen Anne, not that far from Maggie's. The large Victorian had a bohemian feel, which suited Mimi to a T. Done in bright colors, with detail on the carved shingles and trim painted to contrast the cornflower blue of the wooden paneling, the house clearly had the style of its owner.

Mimi answered the door in a flowing caftan that had been chic in the 80s. She pulled off the red and green, as she did all her clothes, with her accessories. Bangles clanged and shimmered as she embraced Maggie in a big hug. Mimi tugged her inside, where she saw Ron and Justin, Ron's new boyfriend, sitting by the fire.

Maggie wondered how Mimi would fare when Justin turned into a permanent fixture in Ron's life. Mimi and Ron had been together for nearly thirty years, almost all of Shelby's life. The pair were inseparable, but it looked as if Justin might be the one man who could pry Ron away. Maggie liked him. The guy had a great job—he owned the architectural firm where Shane worked—a nice personality, and looks, which obviously suited Ron. All that, and Mimi hadn't scared him

148

away yet.

"Hey, Maggie." Ron stood and crossed the room to hug her. Justin did the same.

"You guys look great." They wore matching grins. Such a handsome couple.

"Yes, isn't it disgusting?" Mimi put a hand around Maggie's shoulders. "That they look perfect paired together just makes it worse."

"Too true, darling." Ron winked.

Maggie chuckle and handed Mimi a large bag holding their gifts. "No opening these until tomorrow. And Justin, my gift to you is a massage from Shelby. Sorry, but she refused to give me the gift certificates when I asked."

Mimi nodded. "Girl is head over heels for her new fiancé." She grinned. "We're going to have gorgeous grandbabies."

Ron and Justin nodded, and Ron said to his boyfriend, "I cannot believe you never tried to put a move on Shane. He's so cute."

"True." Justin moved back into the living room. "He's also my employee, and he's straight."

Ron sighed and joined him on the couch before the fire. "Isn't he great?" Ron asked Mimi as he hugged Justin. "So dreamy to have a man with principles."

Mimi made a face at the pair. "You know, not all of us are in love."

"Really?" Ron's purr alerted Maggie.

"What's going on?" *Please don't let them have discovered Mac and me. Not yet. They'll interfere and ruin everything.*

"Well, honey, I've seen our Mimi with a handsome stranger. One that looks a lot your arrogant boss."

"Arrogant, so not Kim." She played along. "You must mean Mac's uncle, Ian."

"Handsome?" Justin asked.

"Don't worry, baby. You're much better looking. Ian looks like a brute. Too many muscles. Just the way Mimi likes them," Ron added.

"Oh shut up." Mimi flushed.

The woman never turned red. All three of them stared at her in shock. Maggie might have worried Mimi was plotting about Maggie's love life, but that blush sealed it.

"You have a boyfriend!" Maggie hooted.

She, Justin and Ron teased Mimi until the woman relented and told them about the new man in her life. Ian Jameson— who would be joining them tonight. *With his nephew.*

Maggie's mouth went dry. She and Mac hadn't been together around other people who really knew them. Those at the gym had seen them working together, but she and Mac hadn't been in an intimate setting together. Could she look at him without mooning? Mac said she wore her emotions on her sleeve. Did she really? Or was it that he knew her so well?

The doorbell rang.

"I'll get it." Mimi danced out of the room.

"Maggie, some wine?" Ron asked.

"Yeah. A big glass," she muttered.

Justin grinned. "You know, Ron warned me, but I really like Mimi."

"We all do. It's just hard to take too much of her at one time," Maggie teased. "She and Ron adopted me years ago. They're good people."

Justin looked at Ron, and she could see the love on his face. "Yes, they are."

Maggie was struck with a fierce longing, a need to feel and see that kind of emotion for someone special. Not a friend or relative, but a lover who would view her the same way. She had a bad feeling she'd lost her heart to Mac. But could he ever feel the same way about her? She'd never had permanence with anyone but Trevor, and he was barely around.

As if she'd thought him into existence, her brother appeared out of the blue.

"Trevor?"

"Surprise." Mimi clapped.

"Hey, short stuff. Did you miss me?"

Overcome with emotion, she threw herself into his arms and hugged him tight. What a very merry Christmas.

Mac entered Mimi's house behind his uncle, only to slam into Ian's back. "Why'd you stop?"

"Uh, sorry." Ian didn't move though, so Mac pushed him aside to shut the door behind him.

He turned around and stopped short. "Who the fuck is that?"

He must have said it louder than he'd anticipated, because the room came to a standstill.

The big blond guy holding a clingy Maggie spun on his heel and gave Mac a glare. He stood as tall as Mac and had a build that suggested he did something physical. Mac didn't care about his size. The bastard was holding Maggie way too tightly.

She saw Mac and grinned through tears. Tears?

Concerned, he stepped forward. "Maggie?"

"Mac, this is Trevor."

The name didn't register for a moment, and then he noticed the same blue eyes and blond hair on the guy. Familiar facial features that on Maggie were breathtaking, on her brother looked ruggedly handsome. Though Mac wouldn't be caught dead describing him as such.

Mac moved to greet him. "Oh right, the brother." He put

his hand out, and Trevor gripped it hard. Mac didn't flinch, and Trevor let go.

"Name's Trevor Doran."

"Mac Jameson." He couldn't help looking down at Maggie. Thank God, those weren't tears of sorrow but joy. "So your brother's in town?" Though glad for her, he felt disappointed too. He'd hoped to spend his free time with her through the holiday.

"I know. Isn't it great? He surprised me."

Trevor smiled down at her, and Mac found himself liking the man.

"Great that you could come back in time for Christmas. I know Maggie misses you."

The room grew quiet, and he glanced back to see his uncle and Mimi exchanging a glance.

"What?" He realized what he'd said and how it must sound. Like the truth, that he and Maggie talked about more than work. "I don't just order Maggie around the gym. We talk some." *And fuck like a pair made for each other.*

"Right. Well, don't just stand there gaping. Mimi, introduce us to your tall, dark and handsome beau." Ron nodded to Ian.

While Maggie disentangled herself from her brother, Mac turned to regard his uncle—Mimi's *beau?* The man had his poker face on, and Mac steeled himself for some unpleasant fallout. He'd never liked that look on his uncle's face, the one that spoke of trouble soon to follow.

Justin tapped Mac on the shoulder. "Beer?" He held out a cold bottle.

"Thanks." Mac took a long drag, waiting.

"Hell." Ian wrapped an arm around Mimi and smiled.

Mac stared in shock. He noticed Maggie's jaw drop as well.

Good to know Mac wasn't the only one surprised.

"Ian and I are dating," Mimi announced.

"That's, uh, that's great?" Maggie offered.

"So you think you can put up with her?" Trevor asked and laughed.

"Trevor, really." Mimi sniffed. "Ian's a perfect gentleman."

Mac coughed. "Wait. My uncle? A gentleman?"

"Shut up, Top." Ian kissed Mimi on the cheek. "This dear girl is precious to me."

"Oh God." Mac didn't know if he could handle all the drama that came with Shane's future mother-in-law. He liked Mimi, but from what he'd heard, dealing with her on a daily basis would drive him nuts. Hell, even Maggie had admitted the same.

"Top?" Maggie squeezed next to him. She looked so damn beautiful wearing a soft red sweater and black slacks. She'd clipped her hair up in a comb that left strands to tickle the neck of her sweater, which hid the love bites he'd left the last time they'd played.

He smiled and met her grin, knowing she'd guessed the direction of his thoughts, because she tugged on the high neck. Before he could answer, Trevor did for him.

"Top is a nickname for a Master Sergeant in the Marine Corps." Trevor came to stand next to Maggie and assessed him. "You look military."

"Yeah." Mac gave Trevor a long look and met the hard glint in his eyes. "So do you."

Maggie crossed her arms over her chest and studied her brother. "Not *my* brother," Maggie said as if she didn't believe that for a second. She gave Trevor a fake smile. "He's an investment banker. I mean, does this big ape look like he could handle danger in foreign countries? Are those the hands of a man used to handling a weapon or a keyboard?" It was obvious to Maggie, apparently, that her brother worked at a dangerous job.

Trevor's backpedaling would have been funny if Mac hadn't sensed Maggie's anger.

"Now Maggie. You know I got these calluses from lifting weights. I'm an investment banker who happens to do work occasionally for Uncle Sam. Government contracts, honey. That's it."

"Really?" Mac had felt the hard skin on the man's trigger finger and middle finger, the callous at the V of his hand, where he no doubt often held a pistol.

"Really," Trevor said with a hard growl.

"Now, now. It's Christmas." Ron tugged them into the living room. "Sit and be merry before I get unpleasant."

"You'd better do it." Justin downed his beer. "The man doesn't look it, but he can get pretty ugly if he doesn't get his way."

Ron flashed a brilliant smile. "True. Mimi, drag in your new man and tell us all about him. How did you two meet, and how long has this been going on?"

Mac crossed his arms over his chest. Just what he'd like to know.

His uncle answered all of Ron's questions easily. Too easily. Mac had that itch that had always forewarned him of danger. He had a feeling his uncle and Mimi coming together had more to do with him and Maggie than them coupling up.

But to his bemusement, he didn't think he minded. The panic he should have felt over the pair trying to fix him and Maggie up didn't appear. He knew Mimi had plans for Maggie, the same way she'd once had plans for Shelby. And Shelby now had a fiancé. Shane, his good buddy, was totally in love with

154

her.

At the thought, he met Maggie's gaze. Those sky-blue eyes sucked him in and refused to let go. Man, he liked just looking at her. Seeing her laugh or smile, watching her go toe-to-toe with some asshole while she dressed him down. She'd somehow burrowed under his skin and into his heart without him realizing she'd been on her way there.

"Hey, jarhead, you want to help me grab something from my car?" Trevor asked, staring from him to Maggie with suspicion.

"Sure. Why not?"

Maggie, he liked. The brother? He didn't yet know. "Be right back," he told his uncle, who waved him away and continued waxing quixotic about his destined first meeting with Mimi at the gym.

Once outside in the cold wind, he and Trevor stood behind a black SUV. Mac sighed. "Well?"

"What's with you and my sister?"

"What's it to you?"

Trevor stared at him. "You dating?"

"Again, what's it to you? She's a big girl, and you're never around to protect her, so what do you care?"

Trevor scowled. "I have a job."

"Yeah? So do I. It's not the one I want, but it's helping my uncle out, so what the hell, I do it."

Trevor said nothing for a moment. "She seems happy. Mimi tells me she's doing well, working at a gallery and your gym, apparently." Trevor widened his stance and crossed his arms. The ass acted as if he didn't feel the cold.

Mac, on the other hand, felt every bit of it. His knee ached, and he wanted nothing more than to go back inside and be with Maggie. But if her big brother wanted a confrontation, so be it. He waited.

"Well?"

"Well what?" Mac asked.

"Are you taking advantage of her or what?"

Mac had to laugh. "You're kidding, right? You do know your sister, don't you? Maggie works for me because she wants to, not because she has to. The woman wraps every guy she knows around her finger by batting those big, baby-blue eyes." He scoffed, but inside, he knew she'd already done the same to him. She'd entrusted him with her secrets, with her desires. His little sub owned his heart, as much as he wished it weren't so.

The truth about sunk him to his knees.

"You have a point." Trevor studied him. "I don't like being away from her so much, but it's what I do."

"And it's dangerous." Mac didn't need to ask specifics. He could read the truth in Trevor's frame, his stance, the way he measured everything around him as if prepared to defend himself. "She loves you, you know. All that sappy orphan crap makes her worry about you even if she won't say it."

Trevor grinned, and it made the guy look even more like Maggie. "Orphan crap?" He laughed. "You say that to my sister?"

"Sure. I'm not going to pity her because she had a rough childhood. You want my opinion, it gave her a leg up. That woman is mean."

Trevor's grin widened. "Yeah, she is, isn't she?"

"She gives me shit all the time." Mac smiled thinking about it. "She's always telling me what to do, and I'm the boss. You'd think because she's little that she'd be easier to work around, but she's not."

He paused in thought, wishing he felt better about loving her. The dreaded L word.

What if she ditched him too? He didn't have the best track record when it came to women. First his mother, then Julie. Now he felt himself loving again for the first time in years. What would stop her from ripping out his heart and stomping on it?

"No, she's not easy to deal with," Trevor said quietly.

Mac didn't know what had happened, but her brother put out his hand.

"Sorry," Trevor apologized. "I'm protective and it seems I don't need to be. Truce?"

"Ah, sure." Mac shook his hand, and this time there was no contest, just a meeting of two men who wanted the best for Maggie.

"Let's go back in and see if we can rattle your uncle. The man wants to date Mimi. He's gotta have brass balls, I tell you."

Mac chuckled. "He was Corps too."

"Yeah? Figures. He'll need to be strong to handle her." Trevor walked with him back to the house. "Some women are like that. Make you work for them, but there's that payoff at the end."

"Payoff?"

Trevor smiled sadly, and just that quickly, the sorrow vanished. "When they say *I love you* and mean it, you know you've struck gold." Trevor punched him in the arm. "So don't blow it, jarhead. Or after Maggie's through gelding you, I'll take a shot at making your life miserable."

"Oh yeah. You're definitely related." Mac followed him inside and joined in the laughter and joy of the holiday.

But as he smiled with the others, his gaze continued to meet Maggie's.

He couldn't help but wonder if he'd made a mistake by not pulling back when he'd had the chance. Now, he knew, it was too late. He'd fallen in love.

CHAPTER THIRTEEN

MAGGIE COULDN'T BELIEVE HER BROTHER HAD SHOWN up on Christmas Eve. As if Santa himself had heard her wishes and made them come true, she was fortunate enough to spend the evening with her family and friends. And Mac, the man who'd come to mean so much to her.

She took Trevor home with her and spent the night on her couch, forcing his big body into her bed, where he'd fit. She hadn't had more than a brief moment to wish Mac a merry Christmas before she and Trevor had left Mimi's. With everyone seeming to watch her and Mac like a hawk, they'd had little interaction together.

But wow, when he'd grazed her hand or nudged her thigh with his on the couch, she'd thought she'd go up in flames. After being with him and making love, the days spent without him next to her felt like months. She felt stupid for such a reaction, especially since two days apart was nothing. Still, the sense of loss persisted. She fell asleep wondering if he missed her as much as she missed him.

Christmas came all too soon, and her brother woke her

Marie Harte

with a steaming mug of coffee.

"Oh, it truly is Christmas. I don't have to make the stuff myself."

He grinned and waved it under her nose. "Merry Christmas, Maggie. I missed you."

Her eyes filled, and she sat up and hugged him tight.

"Easy. I don't want to accidentally give you third degree burns and have to explain myself to your bruiser of a boss." He watched her face and sighed. "So, short stuff, want to tell me about the guy with muscles on top of muscles who watched you like a kid eyeing a stick of candy all night long?"

She flushed, secretly pleased Mac had paid her the attention. "He's, um, my boss."

"I know. He said you're mean."

She frowned. "I am not. He said that?"

Trevor nodded. "Yep. Said you're not easy to work around. I think he likes you. How do you feel about him?"

I'm afraid I love him. She swallowed hard. "He's okay, I guess. Now can I have that coffee?" He handed it to her, and she took it with thanks. "Just the way I like it, light and sweet."

"Unlike your boyfriend," Trevor muttered.

"Excuse me?"

"Oh hell. He watched you the way a hungry dog eyes a bone. He had to have made a move on you already. You're cute, and he's the type."

"I know you're not acting all protective over me within twenty-four hours of you being home. On Christmas."

Trevor groaned and sat on the table across from her. "I love you, Maggie. I missed you a lot this last trip." He paused. "I've decided I need a change. I'm moving back here."

She froze, then put her coffee down slowly. "You mean it? You're moving back to Seattle?"

160

"For good. Oomph." He caught her before they both fell off the table and accepted the hug she forced on him. "Nice to know you're no longer calling me names."

"Like liar and secret government spy and hero for hire?"

"Yeah, like those," he said drily.

She sat back on the couch. "Trevor, I know you do dangerous work. I love you, and I worried for you. I just want you to be safe and happy."

A shadow crossed his face, but she knew better than to pry. Trevor was a lot like Mac in many ways. Stubborn, protective, and he'd only say what he wanted when he wanted, and not before.

"I'll be happy here with you." He smiled at her, and the lost look in his eyes vanished.

"So what will you do now that you're back?"

He shrugged. "I have a few things in mind. A friend of mine is in charge of a big security firm in town. He needs some muscle." At her look, he amended, "Brain muscle."

She scoffed, "Yeah, right. Look, I give up with trying to nag you into being a boring desk man. I'm just glad to have you home, finally."

"But too late to nab Shelby. Damn." He winked. "I hear she's engaged. It's all Mimi would talk about last night, when she wasn't cozying up to Ian. Poor bastard."

Maggie laughed. "Yeah. Scary. But if anyone can handle her, I'm sure it's Ian. He's a tough one."

"Like his nephew, hmm?"

"Oh be quiet. It's Christmas. Now where's my present?"

Later in the evening, after Maggie and Trevor left Shane's Christmas party, they returned home. The party had been a blast. Everyone celebrated Shane and Shelby getting engaged, and Mac and Maggie could smile at each other and be close without setting off any alarm bells, or so she'd assumed. At home after a rousing six hours of extended family time, Trevor begged off, claiming jet lag, but Maggie knew he was giving her the easy way out. She left him alone and headed to Mac's house, her gifts in tow.

She knocked on the door after double-checking the text he'd sent her. Eight on the dot, and she'd come alone. Funny guy.

He opened the door and dragged her inside. Before she could say anything, he shut the door, plucked the bag from her hand, and set it aside before kissing the breath out of her. He had her tight against him, pushing his erection into her belly with insistence.

After he broke the kiss, he continued to nibble at her mouth. "Oh man. I've been dying to do that all day."

"Me too." She circled her arms around his neck and toyed with his nape.

He closed his eyes and moaned. "I love when you do that."

"I know." She grinned at him and swore when he lifted her off her feet. "Hey!"

"You're so little, but you have such a big mouth. Sometimes I forget how easy it is to move you around." He pulled her waist in so that he rubbed against the juncture of her thighs. "Like when I'm moving you up and down over my cock."

She shivered. "Mer-ry Christmas."

He chuckled and kissed her again. "I got you something."

"I know. I feel it."

"No, you idiot. A present."

She blinked at him. "I love presents. Really? For me?"

162

"Yes." He sighed and let her slide down him to the floor. "But we're getting back to this real soon."

"Yes, Sir."

"Not yet." He blew out a breath when she gripped him through his jeans. "You make me come in my pants, you won't sit for a week."

She grinned and reached for the bag holding his gifts.

"No, wait." He left and came back with a small box wrapped in red paper. As he handed it to her, he seemed nervous, and she wondered what the heck he'd gotten her. The box looked to be the same size as the one that had held the nipple clamps. Had he bought her jewelry? More clamps? A ring?

Her heart stopped.

"Look. If you don't like it, we can exchange it. It's no big deal."

She opened the delicate tissue paper and saw a black velvet jeweler's box. She swallowed hard then opened it. Inside sat two sparkling sapphire earrings, encrusted with what looked like diamonds. No, had to be cubic zirconia and blue topaz or something. The things looked incredibly expensive.

She stared at them, loving the shape and design. They looked familiar, but she couldn't place them. "They're beautiful. Where did you get them?"

He seemed relieved. "Put them on." He watched while she put them on and nodded. "She said you'd like them."

"Who?"

"Kim. I wanted to get you something you'd like, but I knew if I asked Shelby, you'd find out. She'd tell Shane, and that big mouth can't keep a secret to save his life."

Maggie gaped. "You asked Kim what I'd like?" He'd gone to the trouble of asking a friend about her?

"She helped me out with a few ideas. So I called some guy and he made you these. I hope they're okay."

She touched the earrings, incredibly moved. "They're amazing." She stood, stunned, when she realized why she recognized the earrings. She'd seen a similar pair of amethyst earrings in the gallery. Steve Zeroi, a talented designer whose work had been on display at The Beholder, had crafted a pair that sold for over a thousand dollars. Maggie had loved the amethyst set but couldn't afford even the thought of buying them. And Mac had gotten Steve to make her a pair?

"It's no big deal." Mac looked uncomfortable, and she couldn't help falling in complete and utter love. The big braggart she'd once thought him to be flushed over spending serious cash on earrings for his kind-of girlfriend. He could have bragged about how much they'd cost, because Steve didn't do costume jewelry. He only used real gems. Holy crap, this must have cost a fortune. And Mac had bought them, had them made, for her.

She kissed him for all she was worth, and they broke apart, panting.

"So I guess this means I'll get a blowjob tonight after all?"

She poked him when he laughed. "Jerk. Now go and sit still for my present. It's two parts, actually. Nothing as grand as this, but I hope you like it."

"Maggie, I'll like anything you got me." He toyed with a strand of her hair, the look in his eyes almost loving. "You're so beautiful." He brought her in for a kiss. "The earrings look good on you."

Because she thought she might cry, she broke contact and teased, "Of course they do. Everything looks good on me."

"Nice ego." He snorted and sat down on the couch. He leaned back and spread his legs wide, giving her ample view of the arousal he couldn't hide.

She loved knowing she made him that way. It boosted her confidence and made her feel like a real woman. Mac's woman.

She grabbed her bag and drew out the present she'd wrapped. She was saving her other present, namely herself, for last. "Okay. If you don't like it, it's fine. I can take it back. Or I can get you something else. Don't feel like you have to take it or anything. I—"

"Jesus. Give me the thing already," Mac growled. He took the box in his hands and felt along the wrapping. "Hmm. Feels like a picture. Like something framed."

"Don't ruin it by guessing. Just open it."

He grinned. "So impatient." Then he carefully opened the paper one end at a time, pulling the tape from the wrapping. God forbid Mac do something disorderly like rip open the package. He slid the frame out and said nothing for a moment.

On pins and needles, she waited for a reaction. It was the last piece she'd given Kim, but she'd changed her mind and swapped it with something else. It was her best, and she wanted Mac to have it. Stupid, but she'd decided to give her red piece to Kim instead. The one that used to hang above her fireplace now sat in The Beholder, waiting for Kim's East Coast contact to swing by and take a look at it.

Mac studied the sculpture framed in glass. A fusion of warm colors with cool undertones at the edges came in to center on a spotlight of gnarled texture that captured the golden blaze of a setting sun. She'd thought of Mac, strong at his core, yet surrounded by facets of cooler temperament and caring selflessness. A charming mishmash of power and subtlety.

He still said nothing.

She felt stupid. "I'll take it back."

165

"Nope. It's mine." He placed it on the side table.

"That's it? It's mine?"

He cocked a brow. "I don't know art, remember? A moron like me would never be able to adequately acknowledge the beauty and grace of a piece of art so exquisite it makes me want to cry."

She blinked at him. "Who are you and what have you done with Mac Jameson?" What he'd said stole her breath away. "Did you mean it?"

"Mean what?" he said gruffly. "I told you I don't know art. I just know what I like. I like it a lot." He pulled her into his lap. "Almost as much as I like you."

She let him draw her down and kiss her. But she didn't know what to think. Though he continued to remain aroused beneath her, the kisses he gave her were tender, heartfelt. Nothing erotic, but genuinely warm. And then he hugged her, putting her face right up against her heart.

"I love it, okay? You gave it to me, and it's mine. No takebacks."

She chuckled, her laughter muffled against his chest. "Don't you want the rest of your present?"

He pulled back to question her. "There's more? I only got you the earrings. Don't tell me I have to go out and buy *more*."

"Ass."

He leered at her. "Keep those insults coming, sweetheart…until we enter our zone. Then it's all about, 'Yes, Sir. No, Sir.' I fucking *love* that."

Then he was going to be ecstatic about her next present.

"Okay. Wait here. I'll bring it to you."

"Fine."

"No peeking. Turn down the lights and rev up that fire, will you? I want the mood to be just right."

"Keep it up with the attitude and you'll pay," he taunted as he left the couch and turned to the fire.

She grabbed her bag and raced into the bathroom down the hall. There, she got naked and dug into the presents she'd wrapped to mask her gift. She pulled the silken corset out and put it on. The red material was laced in black. It barely covered her nipples and plumped her breasts to make them look fuller. Cinched at her waist, the flare that hit her hips ended at the sides but had a flap that narrowly covered her mons and buttoned behind her on her lower back, effectively shielding her crotch unless pulled aside or unbuttoned. The thin string between her ass cheeks could barely be called a thong. More like dental floss made of silk.

She hoped he'd like the outfit. She put on the shoes, then fiddled with her hair in the mirror. She decided to leave the earrings on and left her hair in the clip she wore. Then she donned the fuzzy heels and put a garter on her left thigh. After applying some eye liner, a hint of shadow, and deep red lipstick, she felt ready. Sexy. She fingered the velvet choker collar she'd bought but wondered if it would be too much.

Then she said to hell with it and attached it around her throat. To the small loop on the collar, she fixed a thin velvet lead. Symbolic of ownership if not practical for use, the collar and chain would give Mac a thrill and not make him laugh...she hoped.

Maggie pushed the door open. "You ready?"

"I'm falling asleep in here. Come on."

"Grouch." She left the bathroom and remembered to walk slowly. A sexy sway of her hips, the tiny steps meant to enhance the view of her calves while she subtly thrust her chest out, to give emphasis to her breasts.

She reached the living room to see Mac with his head back

on the couch, his eyes closed. He'd lowered the lighting to a few candles and the fire, and the flickering light did him real justice. He'd unbuttoned his shirt, and the sight of his bare chest in shadow turned her on more than her sexy getup.

"Merry Christmas, Master." She handed the leash to him as he opened his eyes and looked at her.

She had to stand fairly close, because the leash wasn't that long.

But that didn't seem to matter.

"Holy fuck." Mac's eyes were wide, and he didn't stop staring for a full minute.

She let him look his fill, hoping he liked what he saw.

He dropped the leash. "Move back."

She would have been upset he'd let her go, except the look on his face and his guttural tone told her he definitely liked her gift.

Maggie stepped back.

He stood. "Stop. Turn around."

She didn't wear underwear, just the flap from the corset protecting her lower half from scrutiny. Well, her front. Nothing but a thin string nudged the crack of her ass.

"*Motherfucker.*" Mac's hand on her hip forced her to remain still. He touched her where the corset didn't, tracing her flank, her ass, and the smooth skin of her sex. "You shaved completely?" he asked, his voice hoarse.

"For you, Master."

"Little sub, you have earned one hell of a Christmas reward." He turned her around and skated his fingers over the tops of her breasts. "I see nipples." He leaned down to lick, and she sucked in a breath. "The collar and chain are a nice touch." He gripped the leash again. "I like."

"Yes, Sir."

He nodded at the earrings. "You like the jewelry?"

"Very much, Sir."

"Good." He tugged on the corset and her nipples popped free. "Now stay still. Not a word until I tell you."

She didn't speak, caught up in the lust on his face. He kissed her neck and trailed his mouth to her ear. Then he skimmed his fingers over her belly and down to the bottom of the corset. He pulled at the strip hugging her pussy, so that it bit into her clit. In seconds it grew saturated from the arousal she couldn't help.

He whispered against her ear, "I am so fucking turned on right now I'd come if you breathed across my dick. You please me, little sub. You really do."

She melted against him, so in love.

"Now let Master have his way. Whatever I like." He nipped her lobe, mindful of her earring, and kissed a trail down her neck to her chest. There he stopped and stared. "Take off my clothes. Slowly."

She didn't speak, as instructed, and stripped him with gentle fingers, caressing him with all the love she felt inside. Maggie had lusted after Mac. She'd been aggravated, amused, and at turns pleased with him. But she'd never experienced this tenderness for him before, and she wanted to show him what she felt, deep inside. Her fear of a relationship, of commitment, had no place between them, not when this affection felt so right.

With loving hands, she removed the very last piece of clothing, his shirt. His cock had been stiff the entire time, and he looked huge in the light of the fire.

"Good girl." He picked up the leash and tugged her closer. To her disappointment, he took it off her collar. "Put your hands behind your back."

Marie Harte

She did, and when he tied her hands with the leash, she shivered.

"That's it. Good girl. You're in Master's hands now." He kissed her and tugged the corset strap between her legs, rubbing against her clit and snaking it between her ass cheeks. "Yeah, that's nice. You're wet, aren't you? Mmm. So pretty." He leaned down and took her nipple in his mouth.

He bit down and she gasped, close to coming.

"Tell me, sub. Do you need to come? Are you close?"

"I'm close, Sir," she whispered. "But I don't need to come. I need you."

He stared at her. "What do you need?"

"You inside me. Just you, Sir."

Mac nodded and stepped away. He lay down on his back before the fire. "Come sit on my face." He glanced at her as she walked. "Man, those heels kill me."

She smiled and straddled his body, then slowly knelt over his face.

Mac didn't remove the strap. The canny devil pulled it aside and sucked her clit hard. She rocked over him, needing desperately to come but not given permission to.

"Fuck. You're so good. So wet," he moaned and continued to eat her, sliding his fingers through her cream to lube her ass. He sucked and licked while his finger crept closer to anus, then penetrated.

Maggie was out of her mind. She tensed, trying hard not to explode.

"Please, Sir. I'm too close..."

Mac pushed her off his face. "On my cock. Ride me until you come," he ordered in a gravelly voice.

She hurried to kneel over him while he held himself for her. She pushed aside the strap and eased over him, moaning as

170

his thick girth filled her full.

"Fuck me." He stared at her breasts before gripping her nipples. "Up and down, you little slut. Ride Master like you mean it." He pinched her, and she knew it wouldn't take long. "That's it. Take my cum. You know you need it. Spreading your legs for a big man. No small cock for you. Right, little sub?"

She moaned and threw her head back as she slammed down over him again and again.

"That's it. Oh shit. Come on, baby. Come all over me. *Fuck*."

He let go of one nipple to pinch her clit, and she cried his name as she exploded and ground over him.

Mac let her go and gripped her waist while he pulled her harder against him, coming into her with a shudder. "Fuck me. Oh yeah. Take it, Maggie. All of me into that tight cunt."

"Yes, God, *yes*."

They remained locked, her over him, him inside her, as she caught her breath. The corset's tail bit against her ass, making it uncomfortable to move, but Maggie couldn't believe how amazing their night had been.

Mac blinked his eyes open and released his tight hold on her hips. He moaned when she shifted.

"Don't move," he panted. "Shit. That... You..." He tugged her down by the collar and hugged her tight. "That's nothing, sub." He kissed her and shoved his tongue into her mouth, sweeping her into another wave of mindless desire. "We're just getting started."

CHAPTER FOURTEEN

THE NEXT MORNING, MAC COVERED HIS EYES WITH HIS forearm to block the sunlight, feeling drunk. He'd come three times last night, and though he'd wanted to come some more, he'd been bone tired. The physical and emotional wrenching of his heart had made it hard to process anything more than showing Maggie how much he fucking loved her.

God, that look in her eyes when she'd seen the earrings. The damn things cost close to a grand, but he'd wanted her to have them. And then to get that artwork. He knew she'd made it. It had the same look and feel as her other pieces, but this one was exceptional. Even he, a dipshit with no artistic talent, could tell it was beautiful. And she'd wanted him to have something personal she'd made.

That would have been the perfect time to tell her how he felt about her. If he'd had the stones. But then he'd pussed out and decided to wait. Only to be blown away by the sexiest woman on the face of the planet.

Fuck if he'd been able to think past the throbbing in his

dick, lost in lust and love. That corset, the way it cut into her ass and rubbed her pussy. Her flush tits popping out of the top. Her waist had looked impossibly small, making her curves seem more pronounced. And those heels.

He was raring and ready to fuck again. Shit. He'd been hard-pressed to last the previous night. Talk about a Christmas present to end all gifts.

Mac turned on his side and stared at the wonder of his life. Maggie fucking Doran. He'd fallen in love with her. She complemented everything about him. Her needs fit his; her desires became his. That collar and leash.

He wondered if he should wait this morning or give it to her.

He'd not only had that weird artsy guy make her a killer set of earrings, but a matching choker embedded with a sapphire as well. A decorative collar that he and Maggie would know about but would look like simple jewelry to everyone else.

Mac wanted to keep her. Fuck. To have her, hold her, own her.

Love her.

But he needed to be able to offer her something. He had money he'd saved, but no real path for the future. The gym was temporary. She had her art to pursue, but what did he have except a sexy slave he wanted to keep? For the first time he questioned his value He'd found a woman worth holding, but would she want to stay? Eventually the spice and dirty talk and D/s shit might get old. What would they have together? Aside from the obvious physical chemistry, he liked everything about her. But did she like him without the sex?

He hated that he didn't understand women. If he had, he'd have reasoned out what the hell he'd done to scare away his mother and Julie. But he didn't know, and he didn't think he could handle it if Maggie left him too.

Maybe he'd do better to take it slow. Though they'd been battling this coming together for months, only recently had they started to see each other for more than sex, but for a relationship.

He was startled to realize she stared back at him.

"Good morning," she whispered.

"Morning."

She kissed him, and he kissed her back, prepared for the morning-after bullshit. Would she take back all the tender crap she'd fed him? Now that the holiday had ended and she'd gotten her present, was her enthusiasm for him gone?

Her kiss left soon after the thought, but instead of moving away from him, she continued to kiss down his body.

He tensed. "Maggie?"

"Let me," she murmured against his belly.

She continued down his frame to his hard-on. When she breathed over his shaft, he moaned. But she skirted his dick and sucked his balls instead.

"Yeah, baby. That's so good." He put his hand in her hair and petted the soft blond waves over his belly. He'd dreamed about this, but the reality was so much better. She stroked him while she sucked his balls, and then her mouth covered him, and he forgot everything but Maggie.

She drew him deep, all the way to the back of her throat, and then she skated her finger under his balls and back, where she rimmed his ass.

The gentle touch, followed by her finger pushing deeper, pushed him past reason. For once he was helpless to control himself, and he flexed and pumped, shouting her name as he released down her throat.

It wasn't until he finished that he realized he'd been

gripping her by the hair.

He let her go, hazy from coming so hard, and tried to shake free of his euphoria. "Sorry, baby. But shit. That was *amazing.*"

She smiled at him, her eyes so blue he wanted to drown in them. "You liked it."

"You think? I forgot my own damn name."

She laughed and kissed him, and he tasted himself on her lips. So fucking sexy.

"Now who's the master?" she teased.

He answered honestly. "You are."

Later in the day, after Maggie left Mac's and hurried to shower before her brother realized she'd been sexing it up with "that Marine," Maggie dried off and dressed before noticing the message on her home phone.

After playing it, she had to sit down. She played the message again. And again. Then she raced out the door to the gallery.

She returned home later, in shock and awe that her life seemed to be changing at the speed of light. She'd fallen in love with Mac, and though still alarmed about how much she cared for him, she'd decided to let it happen. Her brother prepared to live close by, in *Seattle.* Her best friend had plans to get married, and the art buyer— who'd arrived a month early—interested in displaying her work at several of the galleries he owned up and down the East Coast wanted not just some, but *all* of Maggie's work Kim had at the store.

With his contacts, Kim had informed her excitedly, Maggie could stop working as a retailer and focus on making her art, not selling other people's. She could do what she loved *for a living.*

Maggie didn't know what to think. She was so stunned she feared jinxing the good news, so she decided to keep it under her hat until she inked the deal in a few days, just before New Year's, when she'd accompany Evan Stringer back to Philadelphia to see his main gallery and talk figures.

More exciting than just having her own show was having Evan back her. He bought art for high-end corporations. Fancy hotel lobbies and boardrooms. And he liked her style. He was talking maybe six figures to commission her talents, and from what he'd said, she would have full control of what she designed as long as it adhered to the color schemes the clients wanted. According to Kim, the man was fantastic, honest, and a hell of a businessman.

When Mac called to see what she was doing in the evening, she invited him over to hang out with her and Trevor. She wanted the pair to get along and see them interact.

Unfortunately, she'd chosen the night's entertainment poorly. The Scrabble game nearly ended in a fistfight...between her and her brother. She should have remembered how competitive he could get. The following night she tried to be on her best behavior, except Mac insisted on a rematch of game night, this time over some stupid rummy game with tiles. When he beat her twice and rubbed her nose in it, she went for his throat. Trevor had to pull her back because Mac was laughing too hard.

He had the nerve to call her a sore loser.

So the next night she left Trevor at home and met Mac at the gym, where she tried to wear him down in her step class. All the hard-core steppers joined in, but Mac refused to fade. He did flag a bit in the end, so she counted it a win. But the people in her class acted as if he'd done the impossible by keeping up with her, and he acted victorious, which made the point of all that strenuous exercise moot.

Mac was still laughing when he walked her back to his office and shut the door behind them. "You're a sore loser. I never would have expected that out of Ms. Sweetness and Light. This is too funny." He pulled a bottle of water out of his mini-fridge and tossed it to her before grabbing one for himself.

"You know, I'm just trying to show you that you're not better than me at everything."

He looked surprised. "Who said I'm better? I'm stronger, sure, but you're probably quicker. You're definitely prettier. Smarter... not sure there, but you're no dim bulb."

"Thanks, ever so much."

"And I'd have to say you give better head than I do."

She deliberately misunderstood. "You've blown guys? Really?"

He scowled. "No, blondie. I meant you get me off better than I do you, orally. Jesus."

She started laughing at the look of disgust on his face and couldn't stop.

He stepped around her and locked the door, then fixed the shades on the windows on either side of it. This late at night, not many were at the gym. So why would he...?

He had that look in his eye, the one that told her she was about to get fucked. Hard.

"Wait a minute."

He shook his head.

"I work here," she whispered harshly, worried someone might know what a locked door meant. But messing around in the office? So naughty.

"I work here too." He glanced at his desk and calmly cleared it. He crooked his finger.

"No." She crossed her arms over her chest.

"Oh?" Mac's grin widened. "Look, Miss. If you don't want to lose your job, you'll come here." He lowered his shorts and showcased a mouthwatering erection.

"You'll fire me?"she asked in a husky voice, totally turned on despite her astonishment at his threat.

"I know how much you need this job, what with you looking after sixteen brothers and sisters. You're so desperate, I can do whatever I want with you."

She understood and had to smile. She liked his creativity. "But this is sexual harassment, Mr. Jameson," she said, keeping her voice low.

"You're damn right it is. Get over here."

God, he looked so thick and hard. She scurried to his side, hoping no one would knock on the door. "But I'm so gross, and I—"

He turned her onto her belly over the desk and yanked down her shorts and underwear. Without giving her a chance to refuse, he angled between her legs and rested just inside her pussy.

"Wet for me. I like that. But not too wet. Hmm, this may hurt." The bastard continued to push, grunting as he worked his way inside her.

Bent over with her legs pressed together, she felt too tight, too helpless to resist as his fat cock stretched her. At the thought of such vulnerability, she grew wetter.

"There we go. My naughty employee wants to keep her job, doesn't she?" he growled.

"Yes, Sir."

"That's right," he bit out as he sawed in and out of her, excitement taking its toll on his restraint. "Would you do anything to keep your job?"

"Yes, anything," she breathed.

"Like what? Tell me."

As she came up with all kinds of scenarios, he thrust faster. She liked his desperation, because too often he took his time while she writhed, caught up in his talented, beautiful body.

"Fuck, you're so hot," he said in a low voice. "God, Maggie. I can't stop. Gotta fill you all up. Yes," he hissed as he pumped again and stilled, coming while she groaned her frustration. "Hold on, damn it."

He reached around her and played with her clit, and before she knew it, she'd spasmed around him, her orgasm powerful, the more so because she fought to keep silent.

When she'd climbed down from such pleasure, she felt him withdraw and return to her with something between her legs.

"Sorry, but consider your workout towel needing a good wash."

"Whatever." She moaned at the tingling in her limbs. Mac's sexual prowess left her limp and sated, every time. She knew how rare that was, and how that track record would probably fade with time. Yet being near him, feeling so close, went beyond sex.

"Only thing better than this would be you wearing those earrings and that corset while I did you on the desk." He chuckled. "Now that would be something to see."

She turned in his arms and waited while he set her clothing to rights.

"You're all sweaty," she complained. "You should take off more clothes next time."

"Hussy." He grinned down at her, and she wanted to tell him how she felt, scared yet excited to confess her feelings. Except she'd want to spend more time with him after she confessed her love, and she had a plane to catch. *Tomorrow.*

She swallowed hard, aware she should have told him before now. "Mac?"

"What's up?" He sat back in his chair and laced his hands behind his head, keeping her caged between his knees.

If there was any good time to tell him, it was now, when he had that happy glow in his eyes.

"I have something to tell you."

"Yeah?"

"In my defense, no one knows this yet. Not even Shelby."

He sat straighter in his chair. "Spit it out."

"A few days ago I got a call from Kim. That guy from Philly, Evan Stringer? The artsy guy who was interested in my stuff? Well, he flew out here early since he has family in the area, and he stopped by The Beholder."

"And?"

"He wants my art. All of it! I gave him the rest of my pieces, and I'm flying out to Philadelphia tomorrow to spend a few days going over details about a showing and what he thinks he can do for my career. Corporate sales, fancy businesses that have money, I mean. This could be my big break. My dream."

Mac didn't say anything for a moment. "So you're going out to Philly with this guy?"

She couldn't gauge his tone, but he sounded less than happy for her. "Mac?"

"Sorry, I just… It's a surprise. I'm happy for you, Maggie." He stood up and took her in his arms.

She hugged him back. "I've been dreaming about being a real artist forever. I mean, I know I'm real, but to make a living doing it would be fantastic. Kim says that Evan's legitimate. But that I should have a lawyer look over contractual stipulations, which I will. She gave me a contact to talk to. But

Mac, he wants to buy my work. To sell to other people!"

He stepped back and crossed his arms over his chest. "When did you get the news?"

Uh oh. "A few days ago."

He frowned. "Why didn't you tell me?"

"I don't know. It didn't feel real. I mean, the guy could renege. He could be some lecher who just wants to get in my pants." When he opened his mouth to retort, she stopped him. "But he's not. I didn't just go off Kim's word. I inquired online and spoke to a few friends in the art world, some prominent instructors who've heard of him. I mean, it's commercial, but it's my art. More than selling to galleries but to big firms who pay big money. I'm so excited."

"Excited, yet you didn't want to tell me because...? Tell the truth, Maggie."

She sighed. "Because I didn't want to be a failure if it turned out he was pulling my leg. Aren't you happy for me?"

"Yeah, I guess. Hell, I'm sorry. I just... I'll miss you when you go. That's all."

A huge admission, and his honesty eased the pain that he might not support her. "I'll miss you too. I don't think I'll be back for New Years." She took a leap. "But do you think you could fly out there to be with me? It would mean a lot. I know it's last minute and won't be cheap, but I'd like you to be there if you can come."

Mac looked away and clenched his jaw. "It's a busy time now. I'd like to go, but right after New Years is when we get our crush. All the idiots making resolutions show up like gangbusters. I'll need to be here."

She felt the tension between them but couldn't help it. "Look, I'm sorry I didn't tell you before. I'm still scared this isn't real, if you want the truth. I've worked so hard to get to this point." She touched his shoulder, but he remained on edge.

He smiled at her, but he didn't look that happy. "So are you thinking of moving out East?"

"Honestly, I'm not thinking beyond signing a contract. That's if his original offer is still good." *But Trevor is here, my life is here.* You're *here,* she wanted to add, but Mac's attitude made her think twice. If she started spouting the idea of a more permanent relationship with Mac, she might scare him off. He was already annoyed she hadn't told him her good news when she'd learned of it. She'd do better to wait until he was happy, then she'd confess how much she loved him. *And,* a part of her added, *you want to see how he reacts when you're gone. Will he miss you? Does he care as much as you think he does?* "Who knows what the future will bring?"

"Yeah, who knows," he muttered. He shrugged and grabbed his workout bag. "Well, I concede you beat me." His grin made her feel worse, not better. "I'm tired, and I have some early work tomorrow. I'll see you later then, okay?" He kissed her briefly before urging her toward the door.

Something had changed between them, and she didn't like it but couldn't help it. If Mac didn't want her to pursue her dream, he couldn't be the man she thought he was. But he'd always seemed to support her. She didn't know what to think, Maybe he was still pissed she hadn't confided in him before, and he might have a right to be annoyed. After their recent closeness, if something monumental had happened to him and he hadn't told her about it, she'd be upset with him.

As they left the gym and walked to their cars together, she continued to study him. His face gave nothing away, but he seemed more distanced from her than they'd been in quite a while. They'd argued plenty of times before today, but this was the first time she'd felt true unrest between them.

She stopped him at her car before he could walk away to his. "Wait. Mac."

He turned to face her.

"I'm truly sorry I didn't tell you. I wanted to, but I didn't want you to be disappointed in me if it all turned to crap."

He frowned. "Why would I be disappointed in you?"

"Because you're so successful. Shelby is a wonder in business. Shane's some bigwig architect. Mimi and Ron are the cream of the crop in the design world, and Trevor has one success after another. I'm the only loser in the crowd, it seems."

He sighed and cupped her cheek, and she wanted to sag in his arms and have him tell her it would all be okay. "Honey, you're not a loser. You're one of the hardest working people I know. You selflessly took a job with me to get dirt on Shane."

"Which didn't pan out."

"Not exactly." He smiled, a real grin that put her at ease. "In a convoluted way, you helped get them together. You help everyone else. It's time you helped yourself, isn't it?"

"So you're not mad at me?"

"Mad? No." He took his hand from her face. "I only want the best for you, Maggie. Sincerely. And you let me know if this art prick gets grabby. I'll break his hands for you." He kissed her, in full view of anyone watching. Then he caressed her cheek once more before turning away. "Break a leg and give 'em hell."

"Thanks." She watched him leave, not sure why she felt as if he'd been saying goodbye instead of good luck.

Mac walked away and did his best not to break through his fucking window instead of opening his door and driving away. He'd finally found a woman he wanted to spend his tomorrows with, and she looked to be one foot out the door.

He drove home, feeling dejected and *re*jected. Not a great combination. After letting himself inside, he locked up behind him and grabbed a beer. He downed it and followed with several more, drowning his sorrows in alcohol. A cliché, but he felt entitled. It wasn't every day he met a girl he wanted to collar and call his own. The perfect submissive for Mac. She liked him calling the shots in bed, hadn't cheated on him or tried to empty his wallet, and was a genuinely nice person. And Maggie looked like a walking ad for condoms. So hell yeah, he'd fallen for her. Only to once again have someone he loved walk out the fucking door.

The ball of self-pity and anger with himself for being such a putz grew. He knew better than to open himself up to someone else. Every fucking time he did he got his heart trampled. But had he learned? No.

He stared at the artwork he'd hung in a prominent spot on the living room wall, where he'd be able to see it from just about anywhere in living, dining or kitchen area of his open downstairs floor space. He wanted to eat, breathe and sleep with Maggie Doran in mind. Except now he'd have to go back to daydreams and fantasies.

Reality sucked major ass.

CHAPTER FIFTEEN

A WEEK HAD PASSED WITHOUT MAGGIE, AND FRIDAY morning arrived. With it came the notion that Mac had lost the best thing that had ever happened to him. He couldn't eat, couldn't sleep, and had barely functioned through Shane and Shelby's New Year's Eve party, which he'd left early. His uncle kept trying to counsel him, as if Mac needed another pep talk. The one he'd gotten when Julie had left had done nothing but make his uncle break down in useless tears.

Stupid to be thinking about shit that had gone down nearly twenty years ago, but old wounds lingered. He realized with some surprise that he'd never had a steady girlfriend in all that time. Lots of friends, some with benefits, some not. Much of his time in the Corps had been on the go, and he'd been happy to bond with male Marines in dangerous places, facing life or death situations. Sex on the side came in handy to relieve stress, but otherwise Mac had little time for softness in life.

Then his forced retirement had led him back to Seattle, where he'd figured on putting down roots. With Shane and his family, then Ian, now Shelby and her family, he'd found a new group, new connections. And Maggie.

He rubbed his chest, wishing like hell he could stop thinking about her. She'd called and texted a lot the first day she'd been gone, letting him know she'd extended her stay in Philly. More business meetings and some lawyer she had to talk to. He'd been too hung-over to answer her call, but he'd read her messages. He'd sent her one, telling her good luck, and to remember to knee that dickhead in the balls if he messed with her. They'd chatted via text about New Years, about the East Coast, what Shane and Shelby were up to. But as much as Mac wanted to let her know how much he missed her, he couldn't say it.

A few days passed, and then she'd stopped sending him anything.

He'd heard a few of her phone messages since then, but it became too hard to hear her voice. He realized the mistake he'd made in thinking he might have a shot at normalcy. And he—

"Christ on a crutch, get your head out of your ass already." Ian shoved past him and made a beeline for the coffee pot. "What's this? Too depressed to even make coffee now? Fuck me."

A husky feminine voice said, "I thought I did that last night."

Mac groaned and buried his head in his hands on the kitchen counter, where he'd been trying to get the gumption to go into work today. Instead he now possessed the knowledge that his uncle and Mimi had bumped uglies in his house last night, in the guest bed he'd now have to burn.

"Hey, honey. How about making us some coffee?" Ian smiled at Mimi, and after rolling her eyes at him, she searched for coffee beans and started making the brew. "Now, nephew, we need to talk."

"Shoot me now." He refused to look up until his uncle

grabbed him by the hair and yanked. "*Fuck.* What the hell, Ian?"

"Watch your mouth. Lady present." He nodded at Mimi, who wore Ian's long flannel robe like a queen playing dress up.

"Sorry," Mac muttered. "I'll go back to bed. I think I'm coming down with something."

"No, Mac. *I'm* sorry," Mimi surprised him by apologizing. "What with Ron getting so cozy with Justin and me shacking up with your uncle, we've all completely left you and Maggie to yourselves. Such a shame."

Ian nodded. "It's our fault. No, make that my fault. If you weren't such a dumbass, if I'd raised a smarter kid, you'd have spent New Year's Eve breaking in the New Year with Maggie instead of pouting like a two-year-old because you can't have your favorite treat."

Mac stared at his uncle in astonishment. "Are you high? First of all, I don't need your help. I never needed it."

"Yes, you do," Ian and Mimi said together.

He ignored them. "Second, Maggie and I had a little fun. We dated a few times, end of story. We're good. I'm good."

"Oh?" Mimi raised a brow. "Is that why Maggie's been calling Shelby asking for advice about you? Is that why my precious blond angel is stressing about *you* and *your* feelings when she should be focusing on her career? How selfish."

Ian nodded. "Selfish."

"Fu—shove off." Mac stood up, not needing to hear anymore. He felt bad enough as it was. Now he was to blame because Maggie couldn't enjoy her success.

Ian yanked him back down, and only the fact that Mimi stood so close curbed Mac's impulse to smash his fist into his uncle's face. They'd had a couple of knock-down drag-out fights when he was younger, but he felt more than ready to take the old man on again, and he wouldn't feel bad about breaking bones this time either. Well, he would, but he'd block off that stupid pity that made him such a pussy. *Shit.* He used to be tougher than this.

"You'll sit and listen." Ian's eyes shone, and Mac stared, shocked to see unshed tears there.

"I know I made some mistakes with you. Your father was a dumbass who took too many chances. Instead of taking care of his boy, he was out gambling and found himself in the wrong place at the wrong time. Mac, it could easily have been him mowing someone down in a DUI instead of going under.

"Then your mother, never a strong person to begin with, left. Good riddance, I still say."

Mimi put her hand comfortingly on Ian's shoulder.

"But when Julie left," Ian continued in a shaky voice, "I should have kept it together more. I was stressed and tired and having a hard time when she took off. I didn't handle things right, and you saw more than a young kid should have."

"You did your best," Mac offered, not wanting to talk about any of this. He just wanted to sleep.

"But my best wasn't good enough. Look son, I'm trying to tell you, I know what this is. People who love you leave you, right? That's what you're thinking. Your father dies, your mother deserts you, then on the heels of that, Julie—another mother-type—does the same fucking thing."

Mac still heard the anger in his uncle's voice.

"None of it was because of you, Mac. And Maggie hasn't left you either."

He shrugged. "I know that. There was nothing to leave, anyway. We're just friends."

"Bullshit," Mimi swore. "You and that girl are the best things to happen to each other since... Well, since Shelby and

Shane. Ron and I did the cards before we got preoccupied with love." She kissed Ian smack on the lips, then rolled up her sleeves and started poking Mac in the chest with each word. "The Tarot doesn't lie. That girl loves you. Maggie is stubborn. She's been hurt plenty. You think it was easy for her to give you a chance? The great Romeo of Jameson's Gym?"

"Mac, really." Ian frowned.

"What? That wasn't my doing. Romeo's not a nickname to be proud of unless you're a seventeen-year-old." Like Geo, who truly fit the description. "And she doesn't love me." Could she? Did she really? Then why had she taken off? Why couldn't she stay?

"Maggie *did* give you a chance," Mimi continued. "She worked for you because she liked you. Then she fell in love with you."

"Love." Mac scoffed, but inside he wanted to flee. He hated these kinds of discussions, and the thought of Maggie loving him scared the shit out of him, because he wanted it so much. "She and I had a few good times. She's a good person." His throat closed up, and his eyes burned. She couldn't possibly love him. He wasn't all that loveable.

"Oh Mac." Mimi gave him a pitying glance.

He swore if she threw her arms around him he'd—"*Hey.*" He rubbed the back of his head where she'd smacked him.

"If you're that thickheaded that you don't see Maggie for the wonderful angel she is, you don't deserve her. She's coming back to town tomorrow. We're throwing her a surprise party at six. I suggest you pick her up from the airport with a damn good excuse as to why you're shutting her out. It's one thing to say you don't like talking or texting, but if you don't show up to welcome her home, she'll know you were just using her for sex."

"I was *not* using her for anything," he growled.

"Oh? So the girl gets successful and all of a sudden you two are done? Is that why she asked Trevor to look out for you? She's worried, you idiot. She thought you might have been hurt because you weren't talking to Shane and we hadn't seen you either. So she asked her brother to involve himself in her personal life, something she's *never* done."

Mac swore. He knew he'd felt someone watching him the other day, but then he'd gotten sidetracked feeling sorry for himself.

"Maggie asked Shelby to tell Shane to butt in. She knows something's wrong because you aren't talking to him either, and she's worried about you. Poor, poor Mac." Mimi kicked him in the shin. "Grow up."

"*Ow.*"

Ian grinned. "Nice one, sweetheart."

"Thank you, sexy."

"Stop. My ears are bleeding." Mac still felt miserable, but his load had lightened. "Look, she won't want to see me anyway. I was a dick about her going to Philly. She'll be happier without me there."

"Oh? So you want nothing to do with her?"

"No, I didn't say that. She and I are friends. We agreed we wouldn't get weird for Shelby and Shane's sake."

"How nice." Mimi smiled, and he inwardly cringed. She looked predatory and scary, for all that she was old enough to be his mother. "Then I suppose I should invite Brent and a few of the single men I know to her party. No time like the present for her to make new friends. Ian, get my phone, would you?"

"*All right.*" Mac stood up so fast his stool flew back. "I'll fucking pick her up at the airport. Send the damn directions. And I'm sorry I'm fucking cursing, okay?" He stomped out of the kitchen into his room and slammed the door. *And that's the last time I'm inviting Ian to spend the night. Jesus, he's banging Shelby's mother under my roof. How pathetic am I that my uncle is getting more tail than me?*

God knew it wasn't for lack of opportunity. As if they could sense his vulnerability, women seemed to be fawning over him lately. At the gym, Megan had become a real problem. His favorite coffee shop and a few local hangouts had netted him more phone numbers and offers than he could handle. In the six days Maggie had been gone, he'd been offered sexual ease from half a dozen women. It was weird.

But he couldn't feel any excitement for anyone but his little sub.

I fucking love her. Shit. As he showered, he couldn't help wondering if that stuff about his mother and Julie affected him now. Was he really letting his fucked up mother and that bitch Julie ruin a decent relationship? He'd served in the friggin' USMC. He could handle a pint-sized blond and the emotional rat's nest that came with her, right? He was no pussy.

The day flew by in a rush while he tried to come up with some excuse for acting like an idiot. In retrospect, being so down just because she'd gone away for a few days made him look like a fucking dick. His *girlfriend*—he thought and took a deep breath—had just been handed the best news of her life, and instead of supporting her, he'd turned sulky and acted like one of her many exes.

Later that evening he sat down at the local watering hole, not surprised when Trevor joined him on one side and Shane took the other stool.

"Well, what do you know, Shane," Trevor said with false cheer. "Pussies-R-Us must be meeting here, because lo and behold, it's the president. Hey Mac."

"Fuck you."

"Mimi called me," Trevor said.

"And Ian called me." Shane sighed. "We're here to talk to you."

Mac groaned. "Please. No more talking, okay? I'm fine. I'm picking up Maggie from the airport tomorrow. Then we're going back to my place so I can apologize and we can have hot monkey sex with leather and chains. Good enough for you?" He glared at Trevor.

Trevor nodded. "Sounds fine." His fist shot out before Mac could duck, and the next thing Mac knew, Shane was picking him up off the floor.

Trevor stared at him with disdain. "That's it? That's all you've got? And you think you're good enough for my sister?"

Mac flew at him. They knocked several chairs and tables around, and only the fact that the sleet outside kept the bar practically empty stopped them from hurting anyone but themselves in the scuffle. Mac nailed Trevor in the face and gut and took a few more punches. But in his state of rage, he didn't feel much.

Then his old bouncer buddy Jonas, Shane, and two other men pulled him and Trevor apart.

"Sorry, Jonas," Mac heard Shane explain. "Woman trouble."

"The blond from before, right? Maggie?" Jonas asked.

"My sister," Trevor said coldly.

Jonas looked at him, then at Mac's swelling eye, and sighed. To Mac he asked, "I'm guessing you're not pressing charges?"

"No. Tell Andy I'll pay for the damages."

Jonas and the others left while they sat at a table they hadn't managed to knock over.

Trevor opened his big mouth and said, "According to Mimi, you're messed up, Jameson. But at least you can hit. For a minute there, I wondered." He paused. "Maggie hasn't said much about you to me, but I know my sister. She likes you. A lot."

"I like her too," Mac admitted quietly.

Trevor grunted. "Stop being an asshole and talk to her. She won't stop nagging me until I convince her you're okay. At first I thought you might be fucking her over with some other woman, but I can see you're too pathetic to score."

"Nice one." Shane nodded. "I would have said it's sad to see a Marine taken down by a petite blond. Especially because she's been nothing but nice to you while you sulk like a baby because she left you alone."

"Dick," Mac growled. His head fucking hurt.

"But then I realized, when you love someone, you can act totally stupid. Because women mess you up faster than any drug ever could."

Trevor sighed. "Amen."

"I don't..." Mac couldn't say it. He *did* love her. "I was stupid, okay?"

"Oh yeah." Shane's smugness was going to cost him later. Mac intended on making him pay. "He's in love."

"Shut up," Mac ordered.

To which Trevor replied, "Don't make me regret giving you a chance to make her happy."

Mac groaned. "Will you two shut up already? All this love shit is hurting my head."

"No," Shane said slowly. "That would be Trevor's large fists. Make fun of my running skills all you want, but I would have ducked and run from that attack. Only to come back with a chair, mind you. You took that pounding like a heavy punching bag. I don't think I've ever seen anyone beat you up before. It's a novel experience."

"Shut up, dickhead. He didn't beat me up."

"This is your best friend?" Trevor asked Shane.

"I know. He's pathetic, right?" Shane sighed. "My boy is in love, and it's hard for him. Expressing his feelings is not Mac's strong suit."

"Oh, I don't know," Mac rasped. "I think I expressed my feelings to Trevor well enough."

To his surprise, Trevor chuckled. "He's got you there, Shane. Well, I'm tired. I'm turning in. I'll see you two ladies tomorrow at the party." He glared at Mac to make his point, then left.

"I don't know if I like him or hate him," Shane said.

"I feel you. But he's Maggie's brother, so I'm leaning toward like."

"And toward love when it comes to Maggie, right?"

Mac groaned.

"I know, I know. No more love talk." Shane shook his head. "Been there, done that, buddy. At least Maggie has no idea what a moron you've been. She just thinks you're bad at communication. But dude, this is her time to shine. Don't ruin it for her."

Mac felt like a total shit. "I know. I get it. I was wrong, okay?"

Shane slapped him on the back, right where Trevor had landed a punch.

Mac sucked in a breath. "Easy."

"Come on, lunkhead. Let's get you home before you pick a fight with someone who lands you in jail." Just as Shane finished warning him, they headed into the parking lot toward Mac's car. He'd had all of half a beer and had no problem being the designated driver. Except Wilson—the guy who'd once screwed with Maggie—and two of his huge friends stood in the way, uncaring of the weather, apparently.

"Better run, Nancy," Mac said to Shane. "I have the feeling dickhead and his girlfriends want to play."

"You see what I'm saying?" Wilson told his friends. "Nice eye, Jameson. Why don't my friends and I give you another to match?"

Shane rolled up his sleeves. "Man, it's been a while since I did this."

"Just don't have Shelby blaming me for your injuries," Mac warned and turned to meet Wilson head-on.

The next day at the airport, Mac felt like a huge bundle of nerves. He'd heard big news from his uncle on his way to the Sea-Tac Airport. Of all the times for Ian to disclose such an important decision, it had to be today. His uncle wanted Mac to take over at the gym. Mac had to think about it. He would have said yes if he'd been asked before Maggie, but now, he didn't know what to do.

She stepped into view looking tired but happy. She glanced around, but when she saw him she lit up like a Christmas tree. His heart hammered, and he knew right then and there that she made everything right in his world.

Before she could launch herself over three nuns and a passel of kids who'd broken away from their mother, Mac reached her and pulled her into his arms. He kissed her long and hard, until one of the nuns tapped him on the shoulder.

He flushed. "Oh, sorry."

The woman smiled. "Love is blind, but children aren't."

He tugged her away from the small crowd.

"What happened to your face?" Maggie asked, shocked to

see his black eye and bruised cheek, no doubt.

"I ran into Wilson again. This time he had a few friends. But hey, problem solved. Trust me." He didn't feel the need to talk about Trevor's part in his bruises if he could help it.

Maggie cursed Wilson in a low voice as Mac dragged her toward baggage claim. It took forever to get her suitcase, and while they waited, she filled him in on her triumph.

But her comment about an alternative plan stopped him short. "Wait. Say that again?"

"Eric wants me to move out there."

Mac swallowed hard. "So are you going to move out to Philly? You lived on the East Coast in DC, right? Probably pretty similar."

She sighed. "Too much the same. My life is out here, and I like it." She gave him a look he couldn't figure out.

"Where the hell is your bag?" He wanted to talk to her in private, away from all these people.

"Mac?"

"Yeah?" She'd said her bag was red. Was that it?

"Do you want me to stay here?"

He met her gaze, not sure what to say. He didn't want to hamper her dreams, but he wanted her to want to stay with him.

When he didn't answer right away, she turned to the baggage wheel. "I see."

Fuck. "No, you don't." He grabbed her hand and dragged her toward the restrooms. He spied a mother and son coming out of the family door and dragged Maggie inside the single room and locked them inside.

"Um, Mac? I don't have to go."

"I don't want you to leave, okay?" The pressure to confess about being a selfish jerk took hold, and the truth came spilling free. "I shouldn't have ignored your calls and texts. I should have been there for you. I could have flown out, you know?"

He stared at himself in the mirror instead of looking at her. He didn't want to see her when she told him to kiss off. Yet he couldn't not look at her.

"Why were you so mad at me?" She stood next to him, so pretty yet confused. He hated the hint of sadness in her eyes, especially since he'd put it there.

"I was never mad. I was scared." He blew out a breath. "Maggie, you have so much going for you. You should make your dreams come true. Be that big-time artist. Live where it will do you the most good. Go to Philly if you need to." It hurt to say, but it needed to be said.

"Why didn't you come with me, Mac?"

"Because I fucking love you, okay?" he snarled.

"Wh-what?"

"I'm a pussy. I admit it." He couldn't believe he was saying all this in a public restroom, for God's sake. "I love you, and it scares the shit out of me. I have a bad track record with women I care for. My mother took off, and my aunt left the same way. I have—according to my uncle and Mimi—a problem committing because I'm scared everyone's going to leave me."

Her eyes softened, and he had little enough pride left that he'd use that.

"I'm happy for you. I am. I just don't want to lose you, and that's selfish. God, I hate myself for wanting to keep you here. I don't… I want to be with you. All the time." He felt freer as he rushed the truth. "You make me happy. No one gets me like you do. You don't take my shit. You're a really bad loser. You're mean. And you turn me on like no one ever has." He swallowed hard. "I love you, Maggie. And if you need to move out East to make a go of things, I, uh, I could go with

197

Marie Harte

you. For support."

She stared at him, wide-eyed.

Someone knocked on the door.

"I'll be out in a minute," Maggie yelled. To Mac, she cupped his face and drew him down to her for a tender kiss. "I have never seen you this scared, Mac. And it's not a pretty look on you," she teased.

He didn't take offense, because the smile in her voice and joy in her eyes took his breath away.

"I was abandoned at birth. I transitioned through foster families, so I know what it's like to be left behind."

He blinked, not wanting to cry and look even worse to her.

"It took a lot of work for me not to feel that same way. I had Trevor, and I had some great people to help me along the way. And then I found Shelby. She's my family. Mimi, Ron, now Shane. And you."

He closed his eyes and let out a huge breath of relief.

"I was afraid too. I dated a lot of losers. Then you came along. Gruff, powerful, domineering. Just my type. I didn't want to let you in on my dirty secrets, but you learned them anyway. My private kinks. How the heck was I so lucky to find someone to accept me for who I am?"

"I do, you know." He cleared his throat. "You're so beautiful to me, inside and out."

"God Mac." She wiped a tear from her eye and laughed. "You have the worst timing. We're in a bathroom at the airport."

"Shit. I know. This is probably the most unromantic declaration of love you've ever heard, right?"

"The only one that matters." She kissed him again. "I love you too, you know." She yanked him to her by his shirt. "Sir."

He groaned. "You don't know how happy it makes me to

hear you say that. Maggie, it's been hell without you here. I'm so sorry I didn't go out there with you."

"Actually, it was good I went alone. I stood on my own two feet. The one thing that's scared me is how much I like when you take charge of me. I worry that I'll like it so much I'll let you take over all the time."

He shook his head. "Nope. I don't have any desire to boss you 24/7. Just in bed, where it's the most fun."

Someone knocked again, and Maggie gave what sounded like a giggle.

"Christ. Promise you won't tell anyone I told you I love you at a public toilet." He opened the door and apologized to a lady with three kids.

The woman stared, slack-jawed, at him and Maggie.

"He loves me," Maggie said simply and hugged his arm as he directed her back to the luggage belt.

He found her bag and dragged it and her to his car in record time. But instead of driving home, he pulled into the closest hotel he could find. The place cost an arm and a leg, but he didn't want to wait any longer.

He ignored Maggie's questions and entered their room with her behind him. Then he tugged off their jackets.

"Here, Mac? You couldn't wait until we got home?"

"You talk too much," he growled.

"What—?"

Mac shut her up with a kiss. While Maggie's ears rung, he stepped back and pulled something out of his back pocket.

"I had this to give you at Christmas, to go with the earrings." Mac opened the case and held a beautiful sapphire choker. "I want to collar you, Maggie. Permanently."

She blinked at the piece. "Wait. Collar?"

"Yeah. Something you'll always wear, like a ring but better." He stroked her collar bone. "I love what's between us. I'm not an easy guy, but I'm loyal. I don't… I've never asked anyone to wear my collar. But I want you to have it, little sub. Wear it and think of me."

Maggie stared at it, in awe of what it represented. "So you're good with me being your sub…forever?"

He nodded.

"Just our little secret," she whispered. "And you're sure it doesn't bother you about what I need? Like, the spankings and the bondage sometimes? The submission? I mean, it turns me on," she said while blushing, needing him to truly understand this meant everything to her.

Mac fit his hand around her throat and squeezed, and she shivered, aroused and in love. "I need the same things only you can give me. This isn't a game for me, Maggie. I need you in my life. In my bed. Telling me what to do at the gym." He swallowed and took his hand away. "Ian finally offered to give me full control."

"What did you tell him?"

"I wanted to talk to you about it first. Oh, and he and Mimi are a thing now. I ran into them one morning at my place. The morning after."

Maggie grinned. "You poor thing. I bet Mimi scared you."

"You have no idea." He paused. "But about Ian's offer. What do you think?"

"You need to boss people around. It suits you."

"You suit me." Mac picked up the collar. "Will you accept this?"

"I do." The words made her shiver. "So are you trying to get out of an engagement ring?"

He chuckled as he fastened the silver chain around her

throat. It fit perfectly. "No. I figured we'd take it slow. If I don't drive you insane with my bad habits, and I can handle you being perky in the morning, I figure we could make a go of it."

"Make a go of it?"

He shrugged. "Get married, have kids, everything." He stared down at the choker. "I've never asked anyone for so much before, Maggie. But I'm asking you."

"Mac." She smiled through tears.

He smiled with her, relief there in his deep blue eyes. "It looks right on you, baby. My little sub."

She touched the choker, and a huge ball of joy filled her. "My Master."

"We have this room. A big bed, all to ourselves for"...Mac squinted at the clock..."another four hours until your surprise party."

"Surprise party?"

"Act surprised."

"I will. But we have so much time right now. What shall we do?" She stripped naked.

"That's a very good start."

"Can I give my master a suggestion?"

"As long as it involves me coming in your mouth, pussy or ass, sure thing."

She rolled her eyes.

"I saw that. Oh yeah, you're in sore need of some discipline."

"Take the job at the gym. I'll move into your place." Was she rushing them?

"You can use the garage for your art studio." Apparently not. He stared at her breasts. "I measured. It has plenty of room to store your equipment, and I could seal it in and heat the place to make it more comfortable for you."

He wants me with him. Maggie knelt before him and took him out of his pants. She licked the underside of his shaft.

"*Fuck.*"

"Yes, Master. We need to fuck. I've been empty without you." She licked and sucked his cock while he rocked into her mouth.

"No," he rasped and drew her to her feet, then tossed her on the bed as if she weighed nothing.

She *loved* when he did that.

"We do this my way." He shucked out of his clothes then mounted her and thrust deep. "That's it. Right there. Yeah. We come together, sub. I love you, Maggie."

"I love you too, Sir."

"Even though you have yet to beat me at anything, I love you," he taunted between thrusts.

Maggie clenched him tightly between her legs. Then she turned her attention to his chest and gave in to the urge to suck and bite his nipples.

She noticed his reaction and sucked his nipples harder.

Mac's thrusts grew wilder, his breaths faster. He grazed her clit with each pass, and she rode the passion between them, conscious that his pleasure made everything better.

"Yes, Master. Let me pleasure you, Sir," she begged, on fire to have him. "Come in your willing sub."

"My *dirty* little sub," he growled and came hard, just before she did.

After some time, she roused to feel him stroking her hair. "Dirty, huh?"

"Well, it sounded nicer than naughty slut." He grabbed her hand before she could slap his chest, and chuckled. "Whatever you are, you belong to me, so it's all okay," he said softly.

"Fuck, but I missed you, Maggie."

She nodded. "Me too." Then she grinned as something dawned on her. "I won."

"What?"

She rolled him onto his back and sat over him. "Ha! You came first. I won. I beat you."

He shook his head. "I beat you, *Sir*. Now I have to spank that ass, because how can my sub look so fine wearing her collar if Master doesn't give her the discipline and love she needs?"

She blinked down at him and lowered her head. But her smile bloomed bright. "Yes, Master. I love you too."

Turn the page for a sneak peek at WETWORK, book three in The Works series

WETWORK

Trevor put his hands on her shoulders, and Emma tensed.

"Your jacket?"

She gave it to him, bereft when he let her go to hang it in the front closet. Now feeling a bit nervous, she watched him with caution.

He saw and shook his head. "Tsk tsk. Trust me, little mouse."

"Mouse?" Offended, she placed her hands on her hips and tried to look taller.

"More like a spitting kitten," he said with a grin. "You're so cute. That gorgeous blond hair, those dark eyes… I want that kiss, sweetheart."

His thick voice sounded demanding, yet he stood there, waiting. Leaving it up to her.

She relaxed. *Trust him*, her conscience told her.

"Well?" he asked, his smile irresistible. "Come take advantage of me, and I'll give you a homemade brownie. Even better than one of yours, I'll bet."

"Oh?" A challenge. She liked that.

So did he, by the sparkle in his blue eyes. "Yeah. One kiss, one brownie. If you think mine is better than yours, I get another kiss. If not, I have to rub your feet for you. And no, I don't have a foot fetish." He made a face. "My sister is big on foot rubs for losing a bet. And don't tell her, but her feet gross me out."

She laughed. "Maybe mine will too."

"Nah. You're petite."

"I'm the same size as Maggie."

"No, you're not." His voice deepened. "Trust me. I don't think of you and my sister as alike at all."

"Oh?"

"Other than that you both have blond hair, you're totally different." He gave her a lingering onceover that brought back her butterflies. This time, in a good way.

Her nervous excitement made her giddy, not nauseous. She closed the distance between them and motioned for him to bend down. "I can't reach you."

"No problem." He leaned down, looking so much larger than her. Then he wrapped his arms around her, not holding her too tight, but supporting her. "Kiss me. I confess I've been thinking about this all night."

It felt like a dream, that a man like Trevor, who could probably snap his fingers and have any woman fall at his feet, would want her. But since she doubted she'd get a second date with the man, she wanted to take advantage of him—the situation.

Flushed and wanting, she reached up and drew his head down. She wanted to sink her fingers into his soft blond hair in need of a cut. So she stroked his nape and felt his shudder.

He watched her, not closing his eyes for the kiss, which made *her* tremble. She didn't back down though. Instead, she pulled his mouth to hers and planted a whisper-light kiss on his firm lips.

Like fine wine, he tasted decadent. He let her lead the kiss, not pulling her closer but waiting for her to do the work. Though he remained still, she had no doubt he allowed her to be in charge. As he'd promised, Trevor hadn't done anything improper, giving her no reason to think he might overwhelm her.

Except he did. The taste of him went straight to her head. She wanted to rub up against him, to feel the hard muscle of him all over her body. Her breasts ached, and her nipples strained against the silky cups of her bra. How amazing to be so turned on by a simple kiss. Maybe she'd been too long without a man. But she didn't think kissing John or any of her regular male customers would be like this.

Trevor groaned into her mouth, his breath hot, his tongue brushing against hers and sending a shockwave through her system. Then he pulled away and leaned his forehead against hers.

"Jesus. Hold on." He took a deep breath and let it out slowly. "You're addictive. Better than your cookies," he said in a low rumble.

Pleasure stole through her as she enjoyed his embrace. So what if her body felt on fire. She knew it was for the best that they slow down. Didn't she?

He drew back and stared down at her, and she wondered what he saw. "Let's get that brownie for you." He turned and went into the kitchen, and she sagged against his couch, needing the support to remain upright.

What a kiss.

Her brain remained in a fog even as he returned bearing the brownie on a plate. He wore a wry grin. "I already had my dessert." A glance at her lips confirmed he meant her. "And I want seconds. Go ahead. I dare you to tell me this is not the best brownie you've ever tasted."

Now curious, she noted the rich color and dark scent drifting her way. Chocolate and mint. Her favorite combination. Well, excluding the heady taste of Trevor. He spooned a bit and offered it to her, his gaze intent.

She opened her mouth and took it, experiencing so much more than mere taste under his watchful eye. Trevor made eating seem like a prelude to sex. Heck, he made breathing erotic, because feeling his warm breath against her lips had been akin to foreplay.

"Well?" he asked and took a bite himself, eating off the same fork.

As she chewed, she realized he had indeed bested her. "This is amazing."

His satisfaction was evident by the smirk on his handsome face. "Oh yeah, it is. Almost as tasty as that kiss." He cut her another bite and fed it to her. "So I get another kiss?"

Again, not pushing, but asking her.

"I suppose…"

At her teasing reluctance, his smile faded. "I'm just playing around, Emma. You really don't have to—"

"No. It's okay. I want to."

The big man trying to put her at ease broke down another barrier trying to keep her from falling for him. For once, *nice* didn't make her want to run in the other direction. Nothing about Trevor made him seem like a push-over. He acted respectful while still being forceful. So different from her past exes.

"You want to? Not as much as I do." He set the plate and fork on the table and guided her to the couch. There he sat her over his lap, positioning her like a ragdoll over him. "Damn, you weigh nothing. You sure you ate dinner?"

She grinned. "Flatterer." How nice of him not to mind her growing backside.

"Seriously. You're little." His gaze moved from her face to her breasts and he sighed. "Not little everywhere though. Not where it counts." He gripped her thighs and kept his hands there. "I'm not gonna lie. I'm dying to touch you, Emma. But I don't want to rush you, and I sure the hell don't want you lighting out of here. Be with me because you want to. Like I said, I'm not about forcing you."

Which disappointed her a bit. She did want to be mastered. But she'd only just met Trevor, and she couldn't bear freaking him out with her perverse desires, only to have him rush to Maggie and tell her what a pervert Emma was.

"What's that look?" He cupped her face.

His rough fingers stroked her skin, arcing little jolts of pleasure where he touched.

"N-nothing."

"Not nothing. Tell me," he demanded.

The bark of an order had her automatically responding. "I don't want you to think badly of me."

His voice softened. "Sweetheart, why would I?"

"Well, I, ah, I don't mind if you want to tell me what to do a little. You know, you could be a little bossy and kiss me."

His eyes crinkled. "I could, hmm?" He gripped her thighs tighter. "Maybe…"

"Trevor?"

"But not tonight. I want you comfortable with me."

Not tonight…implying there would be another time? "So we'll date again and then you'll tell me what to do?"

"Oh, we'll date again. You can bet on it."

She felt warm all over. Happy. So happy she leaned down and plastered her mouth to his, letting go of inhibitions to show him what she really wanted. A master, a lover to guide her and demand her submission. She started strong, then forced him to bring her to heel.

And he did, beautifully. What began as her assertive take on the kiss ended with him cupping her head, gripping her hair, and grinding her over him. She was so wet her panties would need a good washing, and she loved every second of it. Especially because he gripped her thighs so hard he'd probably leave marks. And the bite of pain felt exquisite.

When she finally pulled back, they both breathed hard.

"Damn," he muttered, grimacing when she rocked over him. "I think we'd better sit up."

"Oh?" She kissed him again, loving the hitch in his breath.

"You're naughty, aren't you?" He finally let go of her legs and wrapped his massive arms around her back, holding her close. "I can't wait to kiss you again. But not now, or I'll forget myself."

"What will you forget?" she wanted to know.

"That I'm a nice guy." He grinned, but she saw nothing nice and everything predatory in the expression.

ABOUT THE AUTHOR

Caffeine addict, boy referee, and romance aficionado, *New York Times* and *USA Today* bestselling author Marie Harte has over 100 books published with more constantly on the way. She's a confessed bibliophile and devotee of action movies. Whether hiking in Central Oregon, biking around town, or hanging at the local tea shop, she's constantly plotting to give everyone a happily ever after. Visit **http://marieharte.com** and fall in love.